CBSE

[Central Board of Secondary Education]

ECONOMICS

CLASS - XI

Content Table

Chapter – 1 Introduction

What is Economics?

Economics is the study of how people and society choose to employ scarce resources that could have alternative uses in order to produce various commodities and services that satisfy their wants and to distribute them for consumption among various person and groups in society.

Consumer

A consumer is one who consumes goods and services for the satisfaction of his wants. A consumer is a person who consumes a product or service. The word consumer is often used interchangeably with the word customer. This is not entirely accurate. A customer is a person or organisation that purchases goods or services. They may or may not consume them.

Producer

A person is one who produces goods and services for the generation of income. A producer's job involves planning, coordination and management around a movie's script and writing, casting, directing, and editing as well as finances, marketing, release and distribution. A film producer can work for a production company or independently to oversee film production

Service Producer

A service provider is a person who provides some kind of service to other for a payment. Producer services are intermediate inputs to further production activities that are sold to other firms, although households are also important consumers in some cases. They typically have a high information content and often reflect a "contracting out" of support services that could be provided in-house.

Service Holder

A service holder is a person who works for some other person and get paid for it in the form of wages or salary. A service holder is a person who takes service or can say thatwho is working under someone... means employee and the service provider is the person who gives job means employer.

Activities

There are two types of Activities.

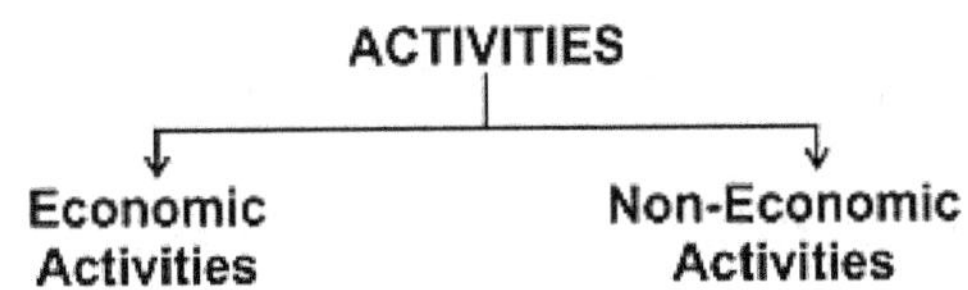

Economic Activities

Those activities which increase the flow of income in the economy are called economic activities. ExampleProduction, consumption and capital formation.

Non-Economic Activities

Those activities which do not increase the flow of income in the economy are called noneconomic activities. Example-Blood donation for a noble cause.

Scarcity

It refers to a situation in which supply of any goods, services or resources is limited in relation to its demand. Scarcity is the root of all economic problems. Had there been no scarcity, there would have been no economic problem. And you would not have studied Economics either. In our daily life, we face various forms of scarcity. The long queues at railway booking counters, crowded buses and trains, shortage of essential commodities, the rush to get a ticket to watch a new film, etc., are all manifestations of scarcity.
We face scarcity because the things that satisfy our wants are limited in availability

Statistics

The purpose of collecting data about these economic problems is to understand and explain these problems in terms of the various causes behind them. In other words, we try to analyse them. For example, when we analyse the hardships of poverty, we try to explain it in terms of the various factors such as unemployment, low
productivity of people, backward technology, etc. But, what purpose does the analysis of poverty serve unless we are able to find ways to mitigate it. We may, therefore, also try to find those measures that help solve an economic problem. In Economics, such measures are known as policies. Statistics may be defined in two main senses.

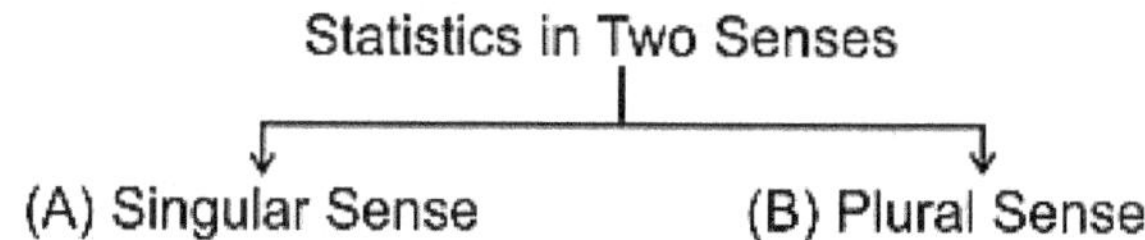

Statistics in singular sense

In singular sense statistics may be define as the collection, organisation, presentation, analysis and interpretation of numerical data.

Statistics in plural sense

In plural sense statistics means aggregate of Numerical facts, which can be placed in relation to one another and which may be affected by multiplicity of causes.

Functions of Statistics:

- To simplify complex facts.
- To present facts in definite form.
- To facilitate policy formulation.
- To help in forecasting.
- To make comparison of facts.
- To enlarge individual knowledge and experience.

Importance of Statistics in Economics:

- Every branch of economics takes support from statistics in order to prove various economics theories in it.
- Helps in understanding and solving various economic problem.
- Helps in studies of market structure.
- Helps in establishing mathematical relation.
- Useful to study of different economic concepts.

Scope of Statistics:

Today the importance of statistics is increasing day by day. Not a single area is visible where statistics is not in use.
In all fields statistics is required whether it is business, politics, banking, economic research etc. For the efficient governance and policy formation data are required to govt. also.

Limitations of Statistics:

- Statistics deals only with quantitative data.
- Statistics deals with aggregate of facts and not with individual facts.
- Statistical results are true on an average.
- Only experts can make the best possible use of statistics.
- Data should be uniformed and homogeneous.
- Statistics can be misused.

Multiple choice Questions

1. "Economics is the study of economic welfare" who said this:
   - **A.** Alfred Marshall
   - **B.** Prof. Pigou
   - **C.** J. K. Mehta
   - **D.** Keynes.

   Answer: A

   Explanation:

Alfred Marshall (1842-1924) defined Economics as "a science of material welfare" in his book "Principles of Economics" in 1890. According to Prof. Dr. Alfred Marshall.

2. Statistics is:
- **A.** Facts
- **B.** Presentation
- **C.** Numerical data
- **D.** None of these.

Answer: B

Explanation:
Statistics is the science concerned with developing and studying methods for collecting, analyzing, interpreting and presenting empirical data.

3. _______ is one who consumes goods and services for the satisfaction of their wants.
- **A.** Producer
- **B.** Consumer
- **C.** Investor
- **D.** All of the above

Answer: B

Explanation:
Consumer is one who consumes goods and services for the satisfaction of their wants.

4. _______ is the one who produces or sells goods and services for the generation of income.
- **A.** Producer
- **B.** Consumer
- **C.** Investor
- **D.** All of the above

Answer: A

Explanation:
Producer is the one who produces or sells goods and services for the generation of income.

5. Saving and Investment are ______ activity.
- **A.** Production
- **B.** Consumption
- **C.** Economic
- **D.** Non-economic

Answer: C

Explanation:
Saving and investment are related, but distinct, processes. Although in common usage the terms have become almost interchangeable, in economic terms they represent two separate activities.

6. Act of abstinence from consumption is known as_____.
- **A.** Production
- **B.** Savings
- **C.** Investment
- **D.** Consumption

Answer: B

Explanation:
Saving means curtailment of consumption or postponement of the present consumption. Thus, saving involves a sacrifice, abstinence or waiting. The rate of interest is considered to be the reward for abstinence or waiting. It is an inducement for the act of saving or foregoing the present consumption.

7. "Economic activity is the study of mankind in the ordinary life of business", this definition was given by:
- **A.** Alfred Marshall
- **B.** Robbins
- **C.** Peterson
- **D.** None of the above

Answer: A

Explanation:
"Economic activity is the study of mankind in the ordinary life of business", this definition was given by Alfred Marshall.

8. Which of the following are Components of economics?
- **A.** Consumption
- **B.** Production
- **C.** Distribution
- **D.** All of the above

Answer: D

Explanation:
Consumption, Production and Distribution are components of Economics.
The process of Usage goods and services for the satisfaction is called consumption. The process of producing goods and services with the motive of maximum profit is called production. The process of distributing income among labours is called distribution.

9. Which of the following can be treated as limitation of statistics?
   - **A.** Statistics does not deal with qualitative data and descriptive facts.
   - **B.** Statistics deals with groups and not with individuals.
   - **C.** Statistical laws are not exact.
   - **D.** All of above

Answer: D

Explanation:

Statistics are aggregate of facts, a single numerical fact can't be called statistics. Thus they only deal with groups and not individuals. Statistics only deals with quantitative data it does not deal well with qualitative data beauty, honesty, goodwil etc cant be measured. The laws of statistic are not exact and they might be used improperly to misinform. Political parties may create misleading statistics to gain favor with the people.

10. Economics is an important branch of which of the following?
   - **A.** Social Science
   - **B.** Development Studies
   - **C.** Political Science
   - **D.** Social Politics

Answer: A

Explanation:

Economics is an important branch of social sciences because it studies human activities which deal with production, consumption, exchange and distribution of scare means.

11. Which of the following are the limitations of statistics?
   - **A.** Study of numerical facts only
   - **B.** Study of aggregates only
   - **C.** Results are true only on an average
   - **D.** All of the above

Answer: C

Explanation:

"Results are true only on an average" are the limitations of statistics.

12. Which of the following is not considered as important for statistics?
   - **A.** Study of numerical facts only
   - **B.** Quantitative expression of economic problem
   - **C.** Inter-sectoral and inter-temporal comparisons
   - **D.** Working out cause and effect relationship

Answer: C

Explanation:

"Inter-sectoral and inter-temporal comparisons" is not considered as important for statistics.

13. Which of the following are features of statistics in a plural sense?
   - **A.** Reasonable accuracy
   - **B.** Set in relation to one another
   - **C.** Predetermined purpose
   - **D.** All of the above

Answer: D

Explanation:

Reasonable accuracy, Set in relation to one another and Predetermined purpose are features of statistics in a plural sense.

14. A _____Statistics alludes to data as far as numbers or mathematical information, like populace measurements, business statistics and so on.
   - **A.** Singular sense
   - **B.** Plural sense
   - **C.** Both A and B
   - **D.** None of the above

Answer: B

Explanation:

A Plural sense Statistics alludes to data as far as numbers or mathematical information, like populace measurements, business statistics and so on.

15. Which of the following about the statistical study is true?
   - **A.** Presentation of data is the first stage of statistical study
   - **B.** Analysis of data is the first stage of statistical study
   - **C.** Collection of data is the first stage of statistical study
   - **D.** Organisation of data is the first stage of statistical study

Answer: C

Explanation:

"Collection of data is the first stage of statistical study" is true about the statistical study.

Chapter – 2 Collection of Data

Introduction

Data collection is the process of gathering and measuring information on variables of interest, in an established systematic fashion that enables one to answer stated research questions, test hypotheses, and evaluate outcomes. Data collection or data gathering is the process of gathering and measuring information on targeted variables in an established system, which then enables one to answer relevant questions and evaluate outcomes.

Sources of Data

1. Primary Source
2. Secondary Sources
3. Published sources
4. Un-published sources

Primary Source

Data originally collected in the process of investigation are known as primary data. This is original form of data which are collected for the first time.It is collected directly from its source of origin.

Secondary Source

It refers to collection of data by some agency, which already collected the data and processed. The data thus collected is called secondary data.

Point of difference between Primary Source and Secondary Source:

1. Accuracy,
2. Originality,
3. Cost,
4. Need of modification

Basis for comparison	Primary data	Secondary data
Meaning	Primary data refer to the first hand data gathered by the researcher himself.	Secondary data means data collected by someone else earlier.
Data	Real time data	Past data
Process	Very involved	Quick and easy
Source	Surveys, observations, experiments, questionnaire, personal interview, etc.	Government publications, websites, books, journal articles, internal records etc.
Cost effectiveness	Expensive	Economical
Collection time	Long	Short
Specific	Always specific to the researcher's needs.	May or may not be specific to the researcher's need.
Accuracy and Reliability	More	Relatively less

Methods of collecting primary data

- Personal interview OR Direct Personal Investigation
- Mailing (questionnaire surveys)
- Telephone interviews
- Indirect verbal investigation
- Information from local sources
- Enumerator method

Sources of Secondary Data
Published sources

- Govt. publication
- semi-Govt. Publication

- Reports of committees & commissions
- Private publications e.g., Journals and News papers research institute, publication of trade association.
- International publications

Unpublished Sources
The statistical data needn't always be published. There are various sources of unpublished statistical material such as the records maintained by private firms, business enterprises, scholars, research workers, etc. They may not like to release their data to any outside agency.

Pilot Survey
Before sending the questionnaire to the information. It should be pretested. As a result of its short comings if any, can be removed. Such pretesting named as pilot survey.

A pilot survey is a preliminary survey used to gather information prior to conducting a survey on a larger scale. Pilot surveys, typically taken by smaller groups, help determine the efficiency of the future survey while also helping organizations smooth out difficulties before administering the main survey.

Sampling

Sampling is a method used in statistical analysis in which a decided number of considerations are taken from a comprehensive population or a sample survey. For sampling, the methodology used from an extensive population depends on the type of study being conducted; but may involve simple random sampling or systematic sampling.

Methods of sampling
1. **Random sampling**
- Simple or unrestricted random sampling
- Restricted random sampling
    - **i.** Stratified
    - **ii.** systematic
    - **iii.** multistage or cluster sampling

2. **Non-Random Sampling**
- Judgment sampling
- Quota sampling
- Convenience sampling

Sampling Error
Sampling error is defined as the amount of inaccuracy in estimating some value, which occurs due to considering a small section of the population, called the sample, instead of the whole population. It is also called an error. Sample surveys take into account the study of a tiny segment of a population, so, there is always a particular amount of inaccuracy in the information obtained. This inaccuracy can be defined as error variance or sampling error.

The concept of sampling error can be understood from the following diagram:

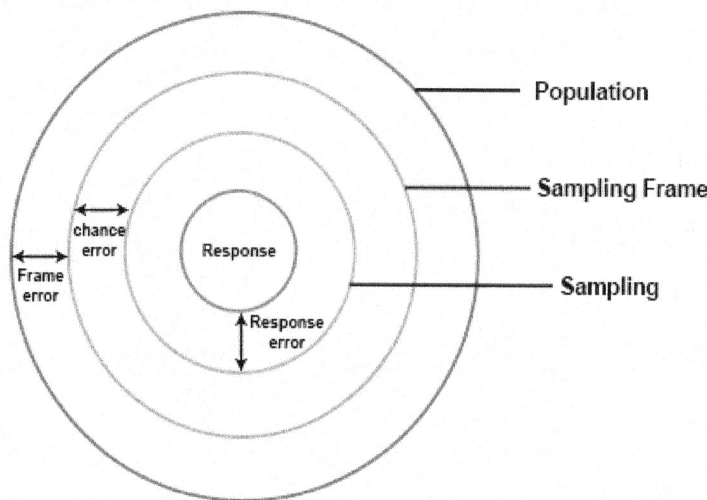

From the above diagram

Sampling Error = (Response Error) + (Frame Error) + (Chance Error)

Sampling Error Formula

The measure of the sampling error can be calculated for particular sample size and design. This measure is termed as the correctness of the sampling plan. Sampling error is also due to the concept called sampling bias. This error is considered a systematic error.

The formula to find the sampling error is given as follows:

If N is the sample size and SE is the sampling error, then

Sampling Error, S. E = $(1/\sqrt{N})$ 100

Non-Sampling Error

A non-sampling error is a statistical term that refers to an error that results during data collection, causing the data to differ from the true values. A non-sampling error differs from a sampling error. A sampling error is limited to any differences between sample values and universe values that arise because the sample size was limited.

Census of India and National Sample Survey Organization

The census of India provides the complete and continuous demographic record of population. This Act was enacted by the government of India on 3rd September 1948 to deal with the legal principles governing the taking of census. This Act applies to the whole India including Jammu and Kashmir.

The NSSO was established by the Govt. of India to conduct nationwide survey on socio-economic issues like employment, literacy, maternity, childcare, utilization of public distribution system etc. The data collected by NSSO survey are released through reports and its quarterly journal "Savasana".

E.g., Size, growth rate, distribution of population, density, population, projections, sex composition and literacy. These data are used by govt. of India for planning purpose.

Census survey

In this method every element of population is included in the investigation. Sample survey : In this method a group of units representing all the units of the population is investigated.

Basis for comparison	Census	Sampling
Meaning	A systematic method that collects and records the data about the members of the population is called Census.	Sampling refers to a portion of the population selected to represent the entire group, in all its characteristics.
Enumeration	Complete	Partial
Study of	Each and every unit of the population	Only a handful of units of the population.
Time required	It is a time consuming process.	It is a fast process.
Cost	Expensive method	Economical method
Results	Reliable and accurate	Less reliable and accurate, due to the margin of error in the data collected.
Error	Not present.	Depends on the size of the population
Appropriate for	Population of heterogeneous nature.	Population of homogeneous nature.

Multiple Choice Questions

1. Which of the following is true regarding secondary sources of data?
   - **A.** It provides firsthand information.
   - **B.** Collection of data from sources who already have collected the data.
   - **C.** Can rely on this data as compared to primary data.
   - **D.** It implies collection of data from its original source.

Answer: A

Explanation:

When the data is collected by an individual or an organization and another individual or organisation use that data this data will termed as secondary data. The objective of collection may vary amongst the investigating and using organisation.

2. Under which method does an investigator prepare a questionnaire keeping in view the objective of enquiry?
    A. Information through correspondents   B. Mailed questionnaire method
    C. Indirect Oral Investigation   D. Direct personal interviews

Answer: D

Explanation:

Under direct personal interview method of data collection, investigators personally visit the respondents, ask them questions pertaining to the enquiry and collect the desired information. By this method more accurate and reliable data can be obtained as there is face-to-face communication.

3. One of the drawbacks of the Direct personal investigation method is _______.
    A. It is very costly and time taking process   B. Difficult to get original data
    C. Questions might be misinterpreted   D. Lacks reliability

Answer: A

Explanation:

Here, the investigator himself visits the persons those are source of the data and collects necessary information either through interview with the persons concerned or through observation of the data on the spot due to which this method is costly as well as time taking.

4. Statistical enquiry means:
    A. Collection of anything   B. Search for knowledge
    C. Search for knowledge with the help of statistical methods.   D. It is science for knowledge

Answer: C

Explanation:

Statistical enquiry means statistical examination. The person who conducts an investigation is referred to as an investigator. The investigator requires the help of an enumerator who gathers data and a respondent who gives the information about statistical examinations..

5. Sample method, compared to Census method, is much better because:
    A. More reliable   B. More expensive
    C. It is less time consuming   D. Carried out by large no of investigator

Answer: C

Explanation:

In the sampling method, a small part of the population can be studied to collect data. Whereas, in the census method, the entire population is studied. Since the sample is very small compared to the population, less labour cost is incurred in the case of the sampling method compared to the census method.

6. A person who actually collect the desired information is called _____.
    A. Enumerator   B. Respondents
    C. Population   D. Investigator

Answer: A

Explanation:

The person who collects data by conducting an enquiry or an investigation is called enumerator. Often the enumerator is a trained person for field work.

7. The problem of doubtful conclusion arises mainly in:
    A. Information through correspondents   B. Information through mailed questionnaire
    C. Indirect Oral Investigation   D. Direct personal interviews

Answer: C

Explanation:

In this method, because the data is collected through indirect sources it may lead us to doubtful conclusion due to ignorance and carelessness of the witness.

8. Data collected by research institutions, scholars, trade associations but not published is:
    A. Collective data   B. Published Data
    C. Personal Data   D. Unpublished Data

Answer: D

Explanation:

Primary data is also known as raw data. It is first-hand information. Data collected or gathered by research institutions is primary data. Because the data has not been published, it is known as unpublished data. Still the data from these sources may be used when needed.

9. Census is:
   A. The method in which data is collected from each and every unit.
   B. The method of planning, organising and publishing data.
   C. The method in which few units out of the entire population are chosen.
   D. The method in which no data is collected

Answer: A

Explanation:
The Census Method is also called a complete enumeration method wherein each and every item in the universe is selected for the data collection. The universe might constitute a particular place, a group of people or any specific locality which is the complete set of items and which are of interest in any particular situation.

10. The method of generalizing data collected from a few units out of the entire population is called ____.
    A. Sample method
    B. Median
    C. Probability
    D. Census method

Answer: A

Explanation:
The data is collected from a handful of population and the conclusion is generalized to the whole population. Concluding the quality of rice by checking only few grains of it, is a daily life example of sampling method.

11. Which law is also called Principle of Stability of Mass Data:
    A. Law of statistical regularity
    B. Gravitational law
    C. Law of Inertia of large numbers
    D. Law of demand

Answer: A

Explanation:
Statistical observations that any anomaly can be discovered by comparing different samples if the samples from a large group of test population trend to group's characteristics.

12. The census act, in India, was passed in the year _______.
    A. 1950
    B. 1949
    C. 1948
    D. 1951

Answer: C

Explanation:
This Act was enacted by the government of India on 3rd September 1948 to deal with the legal principles governing the taking of census. This Act applies to the whole India including Jammu and Kashmir.

13. A person who plan and conduct an empirical investigation independently or with the help of others is called ______.
    A. Invigilator
    B. Respondents
    C. Investigator
    D. Enumerator

Answer: C

Explanation:
Investigator is a person who tends to solve a problem by planning, organising ,conducting, analysing , and concluding a survey. He/She can collect the data him/herself depending on the size of the population and the objective of the survey.

14. What are the qualities that a good questionnaire should have:
    A. Limited number of questions
    B. Instructions
    C. Cross verification
    D. All of these

Answer: A

Explanation:
Following are the qualities of a good questionnaire.
Brief and Limited Questions:
- Simple and Clear
- Unambiguous Questions
- No Personal Questions
- Avoidance of Calculations
- Sequence of the Questions

- Pre-testing
- Instructions
- Cross Examination

15. If an investigator is not able to approach a person listed in the sample or a person from the sample refuse to respond is called:

    A. Errors in data acquisition   **B.** Non response error

    C. Sampling errors   **D.** No error

Answer: B

Explanation:

A non-response error occurs when a useful response is not obtained from the surveys because researchers were unable to contact potential respondents (or potential respondents refused to respond). Because there will be a lack of response in any of the mentioned cases.

16. Following are the method of restricted random sampling except:

    A. Cluster sampling   **B.** Table of random numbers

    C. Purposive sampling   **D.** Stratified sampling

Answer: C

Explanation:

Purposive sampling is not a method of random sampling because some charecterstics are formed to select the population.

17. Which of the following is not the source of government publications?

    A. Annual survey of Industry   **B.** Report on currency

    C. Agricultural statistics of India   **D.** Finance commission report

Answer: D

Explanation:

Union and state governments at time appoint some committees or commissions to make research into any problem such as Finance Commission, Minority Commission, Planning Commission etc. These committees are given a term to probe into the matter. After the expiry of the term, they present the report to the respective authority, which are then published.

18. The statistical data collected by ____ released through its quarterly journal called ____.

    A. DCI, SANCHETNA   **B.** NSSO, SARVEKSHANA

    C. ISO, SARVEKSHANA   **D.** AIS, SANCHETNA

Answer: B

Explanation:

NSSO has been publishing Sarvekshana since July 1977. It has been the major source of information based on the socio-economic surveys undertaken by NSSO on various aspects of national importance.

19. It is a complete set of items that is being studied:

    A. Census   **B.** Sample

    C. Population   **D.** Investigator

Answer: C

Explanation:

Population refers to the entire group or set of individuals, objects, or events being studied, while a sample is a subset of the population that is used for analysis. Descriptive Statistics: Descriptive statistics can be used to analyze both populations and samples. It is the pool from which statistical data is drawn.

20. Which of the following method comes first in collecting primary and secondary data?

    A. Questionnaire Method   **B.** Panel Method

    C. Observation Method   **D.** Interview Method

Answer: C

Explanation:

In observation method, the data is collected from the field with the help of the observer. Therefore, the observation method comes first in collecting primary and secondary data.

21. Population are unlimited in size are referred to as__________.

    A. infinite populations.   **B.** finite populations.

    C. census method.   **D.** none of the above

Answer: A

Explanation:

Population refers to an entire set of people or objects present for the purpose of gathering data and when the population is unlimited in size i.e. it cannot be ascertained easily, it is known as an infinite population.

22. Which of the following is/are not the methods of collection of primary data.

    A. Observation Method   **B.** Interview Method

    C. Questionnaire Method   **D.** Alternative Method

Answer: D

Explanation:

There are various methods for the collection of primary data mainly in surveys and descriptive researches. The observation, interview and questionnaire methods, we collect the primary data.

23. A list of all units under study is known as ________.

    A. type of inquiry   **B.** the frame

    C. standard of accuracy   **D.** method of data collection

Answer: B

Explanation:

Sampling Frame refers to the set of people or objects in the population from whom the information can be collected or who can be sampled for the purpose of gathering information.

24. Primary data mean________.

    A. the data that has already been collected by some agency.   **B.** the data that have already been used by some agency.

    C. the data collected for the first time.   **D.** Both A and B.

Answer: C

Explanation:

Primary data refers to the data that has been collected for the first time and for a unique purpose, i.e., it has not been published earlier. For example, data collected by a student for his/her project.

25. Which of the following operations is conducted after a gap of every ten years?

    A. Economic survey   **B.** Estimates of Foreign Direct Investment (FDI)

    C. Compilation of Human Development Report   **D.** General Census

Answer: D

Explanation:

General census is the official counting of a region's or nation's people and compilation of economics , social and other data usually for formulation of development policies and plans etc. General census is an operation which is conducted after a gap of every ten years.

26. Which of the following is a very costly and time-consuming method?

    A. Mailed questionnaires.   **B.** Schedules sent through enumerators

    C. Information through agencies   **D.** Indirect oral interview

Answer: B

Explanation:

Schedules sent through enumerator is a method for collecting primary data in which schedules are sent to the enumerators and then they collect the data. It is a very time consuming method and costly.

27. The non-sampling errors may arise due to ________.

    A. defective methods of data collection   **B.** defective methods of tabulation

    C. faulty definition   **D.** all of the above

Answer: D

Explanation:

The non sampling errors arise when the data values don't reflects the correct population i.e. researcher may use wrong method for collecting data or the defaulted method of tabulation.

28. When data is classified on the basis of attribute it is termed as________.

    A. Geographical   **B.** Qualitative

    C. Chronological   **D.** Both A & C

Answer: B

Explanation:

When data is classified on the basis of attribute it is termed as qualitative data. Qualitative data highlights the quality of the information. Attribute gets the special emphasis in analysing the data.

29. After doing the thorough calculation of consumer demand by setting up stimulated stores, providing a sample of consumers with money, and then allowing them to purchase and keep the commodities they select in the stores is called the __________.
    A. consumer survey approach
    B. observational approach
    C. consumer clinic approach
    D. product research approach

Answer: C

Explanation:

After doing the thorough calculation of consumer demand by setting up stimulated stores, providing a sample of consumers with money, and then allowing them to purchase and keep the commodities they select in the stores is called the consumer clinic approach. It is also known as 'Laboratory type' experiment. By this approach, a sample of consumers is given a specific budget and asked to plan out their expenditure.

30. Data collected by research institutions is __________.
    A. primary data
    B. secondary unpublished data
    C. secondary published data
    D. All of the above

Answer: A

Explanation:

Primary data is also known as raw data. It is the first-hand information. Data collected or gathered by research institutions is primary data. Primary data is collected only for a specific purpose.

Chapter – 3 Organization of Data

Introduction

Data organization is the practice of categorizing and classifying data to make it more usable. Similar to a file folder, where we keep important documents, you'll need to arrange your data in the most logical and orderly fashion, so you and anyone else who accesses it can easily find what they're looking for. Data organization is the way to arrange the raw data in an understandable order. Organizing data includes classification, frequency distribution table, picture representation, graphical representation, etc. Data organization helps us to arrange the data in order that we can easily read and work. Organization of data refers to the systematic arrangement of collected figures (raw data), so that the data becomes easy to understand and more convenient for further statistical treatment.

Classification

Classification is the process of arranging data into sequences and groups according to their common characteristics of separating them in to different but related parts.

Characteristics of classification
1. Homogeneity
2. Suitability
3. Clarity
4. Flexibility
5. Diversification

Basis of classification
- **Chronological classification:** In such a classification data are classified either in ascending or in descending order with reference to time such as years, quarters, months weeks etc.
- **Geographical/Spatial classification:** The data are classified with reference to geographical location/place such as countries, states, cities, districts, block etc.
- **Qualitative classification:** Data are classified with reference to descriptive characteristics like sex, caste, religion literacy etc.
- **Quantitative classification:** Data are classified on the basis of some measurable characteristics such as height, age, weight, income, marks of students.
- **Conditional classification:** When data are classified with respect to condition, the type of classification is called conditional classification.

Variable

A variable is a characteristic which is capable of being measured and capable of change in its value from time to time.
A characteristic which is capable of being measured and changes its value overtime is called a variable.
It is of two types:
1. Discrete variable
2. Continuous variable

Discrete variable
Variables that are capable of taking only an exact value and not any fractional value are termed discrete variables. For example, the number of workers or the number of students in a class is a discrete variable as they cannot be in fractions. Similarly, the number of children in a family can be 1, 2, and so on, but cannot be 1.5, 2.75.

Continuous variable
Variables that can take all the possible values (integral as well as fractional) in a given specified range are termed continuous variables. For example, temperature, height, weight, marks, etc.

A frequency distribution is a comprehensive way to classify raw data of a quantitative variable. It shows how different values of a variable is distributed in different classes along with their corresponding class frequencies.

Class mid-point or class mark

The class mid-point or class mark is the middle value of a class. It lies halfway between the lower class limit and the upper class limit of a class and can be ascertained in the following manner.

Class mid-point = upper class limit + lower class limit / 2.

Class frequency

It means the number of values in a particular class.

Class width

It is the difference between the upper class limit and lower class limit.

Class Limits

There are two ends of a class. The lowest value is called lower class limit and highest value is called upper class limit.

The classes, by the exclusive method is formed in such a way that the upper class limit of one class equals the lower class limit of the next class. eg 0-10, 10-20.

In comparison to the exclusive method, the inclusive method does not excludes the upper class limit in a class interval. It includes the upper class in a class. Thus both class limits are parts of the class intervals e.g., 0-9, 10-19.

The classification of data as a frequency distribution has an inherent short coming. While it summarizes the raw data making it concise and comprehensible. It does not show the details that are found in raw data. So there is a loss of information in classifying raw data.

The difference between Univariate and Bivariate Frequency distribution

Basis	Univariate Frequency distribution	Bivariate Frequency distribution
Meaning	When data is classified on the basis of single variable,the distribution is known as univariate frequency distribution.	when data is classified on the basis of two variables, the distribution is known as bivariate frequency distribution.
Alternate Name	One-way frequency	Two-way frequency
Example	Height of students in a class	Height and weight of students in a class

Types of series

1. Individual series
2. Frequency series
   - Discrete series or Frequency array
   - Frequency distribution or Continuous series

1. Individual series

Individual series are those series in which the items are listed singly. For example:

Sr. No. of workers	Daily wages (in Rs.)
1.	25
2.	50
3.	35
4.	40
5.	20
6.	45

2. Frequency series

Discrete series or Frequency array: A discrete series or frequency array is that series in which data are prescribed in a way that exact measurements of items are clearly shown. The example in following table illustrates a frequency array.

Size of the household	Number of household (Frequency)
1.	5
2.	15
3.	25
4.	35
5.	10
6.	5

Frequency distribution or Continuous series: A continuous series: It is that series in which items cannot be exactly measured. The items assume a range of values and are placed within the range of limits. In other words, data are classified into different classes with a range, the range is called class-intervals.

Marks	Frequency
10-20	4
20-30	5
30-40	8
40-50	5
50-60	4
60-70	3

Multiple Choice Questions

1. _______ of the data refers to the arrangement of figures in such a form that comparison of the mass of similar data may be facilitated and further analysis may be possible.
   - **A.** Analysis
   - **B.** Organization
   - **C.** Collection
   - **D.** Interpretation

Answer: B

Explanation:

Organization of the data refers to the arrangement of figures in such a form that comparison of the mass of similar data may be facilitated and further analysis may be possible.

2. It is the process of arranging things in groups or classes according to their resemblances:
   - **A.** Interpretation
   - **B.** Collection
   - **C.** Analysis
   - **D.** Classification

Answer: D

Explanation:

The process of arranging data into homogenous group or classes according to some common characteristics present in the data is called Classification.

3. Continuous variable assumes _______.
   - **A.** A range of values
   - **B.** Increase in jumps
   - **C.** Both
   - **D.** None

Answer: A

Explanation:

If a variable can take on any value between its minimum value and its maximum value, it is called a continuous variable.

4. Classification data based on the geographical differences of the data is:
   - **A.** Chronological
   - **B.** Spatial
   - **C.** Quantitative
   - **D.** Qualitative

Answer: B

Explanation:

Spatial dependence is measured as the existence of statistical dependence in a collection of random variables, each of which is associated with a different geographical location.

5. Chronological classification is:
   - **A.** Classification on the basis quantity
   - **B.** Classification on the basis location
   - **C.** Classification on the basis of quality
   - **D.** Classification on the basis of time

Answer: D

Explanation:

When data are observed over a period of time the type of classification is known as chronological classification. Such type of classification helps to compare the data of different time periods.

6. A characteristic or a phenomenon which is capable of being measured and changes its value overtime is called:
   - **A.** Sample
   - **B.** Vector
   - **C.** Variable
   - **D.** None

Answer: C

Explanation:

Variables data is data that is acquired through measurements, such as length, time, diameter, strength, weight, temperature, density, thickness, pressure, and height. With variables data, you can decide the measurement's degree of accuracy.

7. Which variable increase in jumps or in complete numbers:
   - **A.** Individual
   - **B.** Continuous
   - **C.** Discrete
   - **D.** Multiple

Answer: C

Explanation:

Discrete variable over a particular range of real values is one for which, for any value in the range that the variable is permitted to take on, there is a positive minimum distance to the nearest other permissible value. The number of permitted values is either finite or countably infinite.

8. Class limits means:
   - **A.** Sum of upper or lower limits
   - **B.** Difference between upper or lower limits
   - **C.** Extreme values of a class are limits
   - **D.** A range of values which incorporates a set of items

Answer: C

Explanation:

Class limits have the same accuracy as the data values; the same number of decimal places as the data values. The lower class limit of a class is the smallest data value that can go into the class. The upper class limit of a class is the largest data value that can go into the class.

9. Series of statistical data with one variable only is called:
   - **A.** Continuous
   - **B.** Individual Series
   - **C.** Discrete
   - **D.** None

Answer: B

Explanation:

A series of individual observations is a series in which items are listed individually. A series of statistical data showing the frequency of only one variable is called univariate frequency distribution. In other words, the frequency distribution of a single variable is called univariate frequency distribution.

10. The number of times an item occur in the series is known as:
    - **A.** Frequency
    - **B.** Series
    - **C.** Class
    - **D.** Variable

Answer: A

Explanation:

Frequency is the number of occurrences of a repeating event per unit time. It is also referred to as temporal frequency, which emphasizes the contrast to spatial frequency and angular frequency.

11. Which of the following is false regarding discrete series:
    - **A.** Item in the series are measured with some range
    - **B.** Difficult to present large mass of data through this series
    - **C.** In such series there is no class intervals
    - **D.** This series present the data in a very brief form

Answer: A

Explanation:

Discrete data is information that can be categorized into a classification. Discrete data is based on counts. Only a finite number of values is possible, and the values cannot be subdivided meaningfully.

12. Classification like male-female, healthy-unhealthy, educated-uneducated are example of:

A. Manifold	**B.** Dichotomy
C. Both	**D.** None

Answer: B

Explanation:

Dichotomous variables are nominal variables which have only two categories or levels. For example, if we were looking at gender, we would most probably categorize somebody as either "male" or "female". This is an example of a dichotomous variable (and also a nominal variable).

13. How variable is differ from attributes:

A. They can be measured both numerically as well as qualitatively	**B.** They can be measured Qualitatively
C. They can be measured numerically	**D.** None

Answer: D

Explanation:

Attributes assigned to variables may have the same units as the variable or have no units. If you want to store data that requires units different from those of the associated variable, it is better to use a variable than an attribute.

14. Series in which every class interval excludes items corresponding to its upper limits:

A. Exclusive Series	**B.** Cumulative frequency
C. Inclusive Series	**D.** Open ended

Answer: A

Explanation:

When the class intervals are so fixed that the upper limit of one class is the lower limit of the next class; it is known as the exclusive method of classification. The exclusive method ensures continuity of data as much as the upper limit of one class is the lower limit of the next class.

15. The data related with population, sales of a firm, imports and exports of a country are always subjected to:

A. Chronological classification	**B.** Qualitative
C. Quantitative	**D.** Spatial classification

Answer: A

Explanation:

In chronological classification the collected data are arranged according to the order of time expressed in years, months, weeks, etc., The data is generally classified in ascending order of time. For example, the data related with population, sales of a firm, imports and exports of a country are always subjected to chronological classification.

16. How exclusive series is differed from inclusive series:

A. Upper limits one class interval does not repeats itself as lower limit of the next class	**B.** lower limits one class interval repeats itself as Upper limit of the next class
C. Upper limits one class interval double itself as lower limit of the next class	**D.** Upper limits one class interval repeats itself as lower limit of the next class

Answer: D

Explanation:

Under exclusive method class intervals are so fixed that upper limits of class is the lower limit of the next class.

17. When the collected data is grouped with reference to time, we have:

A. Qualitative classification	**B.** Qualitative classification
C. Chorological Classification	**D.** Quantitative classification

Answer: C

Explanation:

When data are observed over a period of time the type of classification is known as chronological classification. In chronological classification the collected data are arranged according to the order of time expressed in years, months, weeks, etc., The data is generally classified in ascending order of time.

18. The data recorded according to standard of education like illiterate, primary, secondary, graduate, technical etc., will be known as _______ classification.

A. Geographical Classification	**B.** Qualitative classification
C. Chorological Classification	**D.** Quantitative classification

Answer: B

Explanation:
Data collected about a categorical variable will always be qualitative. Qualitative data is a categorical measurement expressed not in terms of numbers, but rather by means of a natural language description. In statistics, it is often used interchangeably with "categorical" data.

19. In a manifold table we have data on ______.

- **A.** Only one character
- **B.** More than one character
- **C.** More than three characters
- **D.** More than two character

Answer: C

Explanation:
The manifold data table explains more than three characteristics of the data.

20. When the raw data is arranged in ascending or descending order, then the data is called ____.

- **A.** processed data
- **B.** secondary data
- **C.** arrayed data
- **D.** raw data

Answer: C

Explanation:
When the raw data is arranged in ascending or descending order, then the data is called arrayed data.
Example: The marks obtained by 5 students in a Science test as given below in raw data:70, 100, 45, 80, 55 Raw data into Arrayed data: 45, 55, 70, 80, 100.

21. Which one of the following data is in the form of arrayed data?

- **A.** 23, 45, 1, 89, 20, 10
- **B.** 23, 17, 3, 89, 90, 89
- **C.** 23, 25, 12, 8, 20, 56
- **D.** 1, 10, 20, 23, 45, 89

Answer: D

Explanation:
The last option is in form of arrayed data. Since the data are arranged in ascending order.

22. The number of traffic citations issued during the last 5 months in Mumbai city, is 24,30,12,11 and 7. What kind of data is used?

- **A.** processed data
- **B.** secondary data
- **C.** arrayed data
- **D.** raw data

Answer: D

Explanation:
The data are in the form of raw data. 24,30,12,11 and 7. Since the data are given randomly.

23. The class mid-point is equal to:

- **A.** The ratio of the upper class limit and the lower class limit
- **B.** The average of the upper class limit and the lower class limit
- **C.** The product of upper class limit and the lower class limit
- **D.** None of these

Answer: B

Explanation:
The lower limit for every class is the smallest value in that class. On the other hand, the upper limit for every class is the greatest value in that class. The class midpoint is the lower class limit plus the upper class limit divided by 2.

24. How individual series is differ from discrete series:

- **A.** Frequency for each item is more than one
- **B.** Value are given in the form of group
- **C.** There is no column for frequency
- **D.** None

Answer: D

Explanation:
Individual series are those series in which items are listened singely, discrete series are those series in which data are presented in manner that exact measurement of items are clearly shown.

25. Expression of the class interval 90-99 in open ended classes will be:

- **A.** 90 and above
- **B.** Below 99
- **C.** Both
- **D.** None

Answer: B

Explanation:

If, in a frequency distribution, the initial class interval is indeterminate at its beginning and/or the final class interval is indeterminate at its end, the distribution is said to possess "open ended" classes.

26. There are two class interval 0-10 and 10-20 , if a student score 10 marks then he should be included in which class interval:
- **A.** 0-10
- **B.** 10-20
- **C.** Both the 0-10 and 10-20
- **D.** Not be included in these intervals

Answer: C

Explanation:

This is an exclusive class interval. When the lower limit is included, but the upper limit is excluded, then it is an exclusive class interval.

27. In an examination 10 students scored the following marks in Mathematics: 35, 19, 28, 32, 63, 02, 47, 31, 13, 13, 98. Its range is:
- **A.** 2
- **B.** 96
- **C.** 98
- **D.** 50

Answer: B

Explanation:

Range = Maximum value of the variable – Minimum value of the variable = 98 – 2 = 96

28. The difference between upper and lower limit is called:
- **A.** Group
- **B.** Class marks
- **C.** Class size
- **D.** Class internal

Answer: C

Explanation:

Class size = Upper Limit- Lower limit

29. Which data information can be collected randomly?
- **A.** Array
- **B.** Primary
- **C.** Secondary
- **D.** Raw

Answer: D

Explanation:

Raw data information can be collected randomly. Example: Consider the height of 10 students in a class given below: 55, 36, 95, 73, 60, 42, 25, 78, 75, 62, This data in this form is called raw data.

30. An orderly distribution of the raw data into certain specified categories is known as:
- **A.** Frequency Distribution
- **B.** Frequency
- **C.** Cumulative Frequency
- **D.** Primary Data

Answer: A

Explanation:

The definition of the frequency distribution is distributing the raw data in the specific categories in an order.

Chapter – 4   Presentation of Data

Introduction

Data presentation is a process of comparing two or more data sets with visual aids, such as graphs. Using a graph, you can represent how the information relates to other data. This process follows data analysis and helps organize information by visualizing and putting it into a more readable format. This process is useful in nearly every industry, as it helps professionals share their findings after performing data analysis.

The presentation of data means exhibition of data in such a clear and attractive manner that these can be easily understood and analyzed.

Tabular presentation of data

It is a table that helps to represent even a large amount of data in an engaging, easy to read, and coordinated manner. The data is arranged in rows and columns. This is one of the most popularly used forms of presentation of data as data tables are simple to prepare and read.

The most significant benefit of tabulation is that it coordinates data for additional statistical treatment and decision making. The analysis used in tabulation is of four types. They are:

1. **Qualitative Classification**

   When classification is done according to attributes such as social status, nationality, etc. It is called qualitative classification.

2. **Quantitative Classification**

   In this, the data are classified on the basis of characteristics which are quantitative in nature. e.g., age, height, income, etc.

3. **Temporal classification**

   In this, time becomes the becomes the classifying variable and data are categorised according to time. Time may be in hours, weeks, years, etc.

4. **Spatial classification**

   When classification is done on the basis of place, it is called spatial classification. The place may be a village, town, state, country, etc.

Objectives Of Tabulation

Following are the objectives of tabulation:
- To simplify the complex data
- To bring out essential features of the data
- To facilitate comparison
- To facilitate statistical analysis
- Saving of space

What are the Three Limitations of a Table?

Following are the major limitations of a table:
1. **Lacks description**
- The table represents only figures and not attributes.
- It ignores the qualitative aspects of the facts.

2. **Incapable of presenting individual items**
- It does not present individual items.
- It presents aggregate data.

3. **Needs special knowledge**

- The understanding of the table requires special knowledge.
- It cannot be easily used by a layman.

Diagrammatic Presentation of Data

The diagrammatic presentation of data gives an immediate understanding of the real situation to be defined by the data in comparison to the tabular presentation of data or textual representations. It translates the highly complex ideas included in numbers into a more concrete and quickly understandable form pretty effectively. Diagrams may be less certain but are much more efficient than tables in displaying the data.

Types of Diagrammatic Presentation

1. **Geometric Form**
- Pie Diagram
- Bar Diagram
    - Simple
    - Multiple
    - Sub Divided
    - Percentage

2. **Frequency Diagram**
- Histogram
- Frequency Polygon
- Frequency Curve
- Ogive curve

3. **Arithmetic Line Graph or Time series graph**
- **Bar diagram:** Bar diagrams are those diagrams in which data are presented in the form of bars or rectangles.

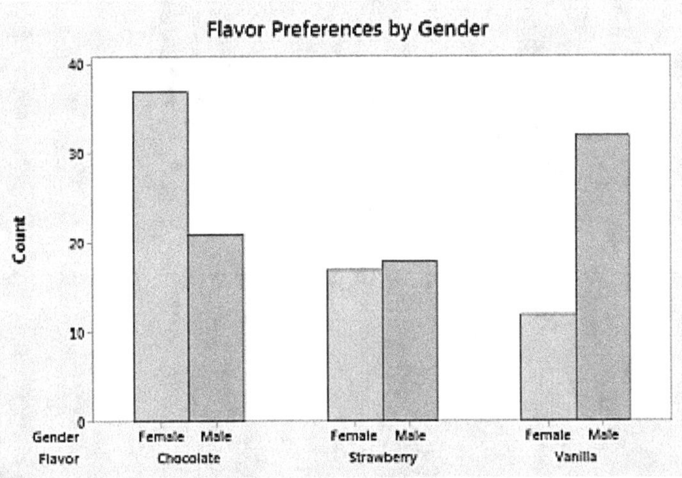

- **Simple bar diagram:** They are those diagrams which are based on a single set of numerical data. Different items are represented by different bars.

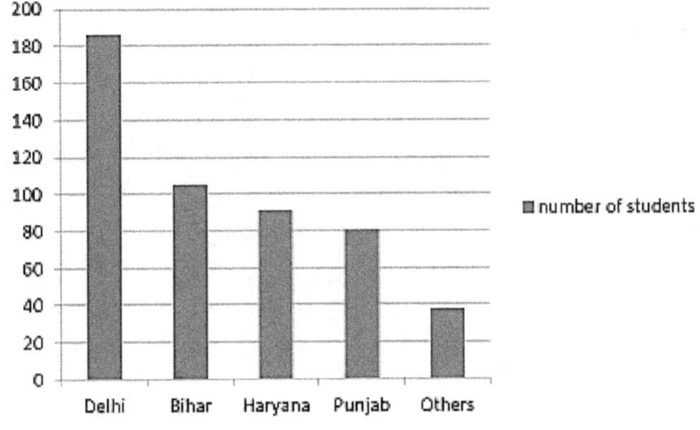

- **Multiple bar diagram:** They are those diagrams which show two or more sets of data simultaneously. This type of diagram is, generally, used to make comparison between two sets of series.

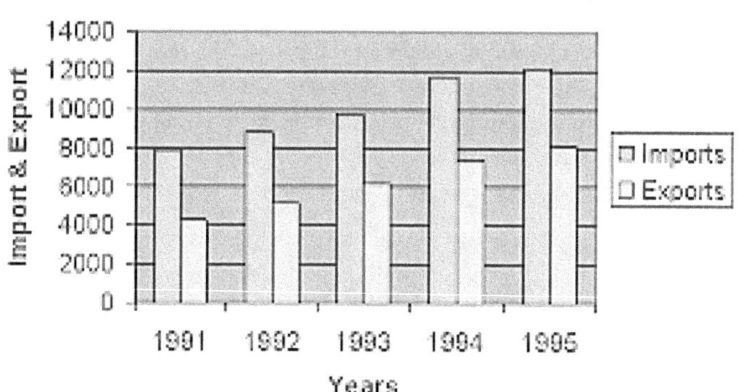

- **Sub divided bar diagram:** These are those diagrams which present simultaneously, total values and parts there in a set of a data.

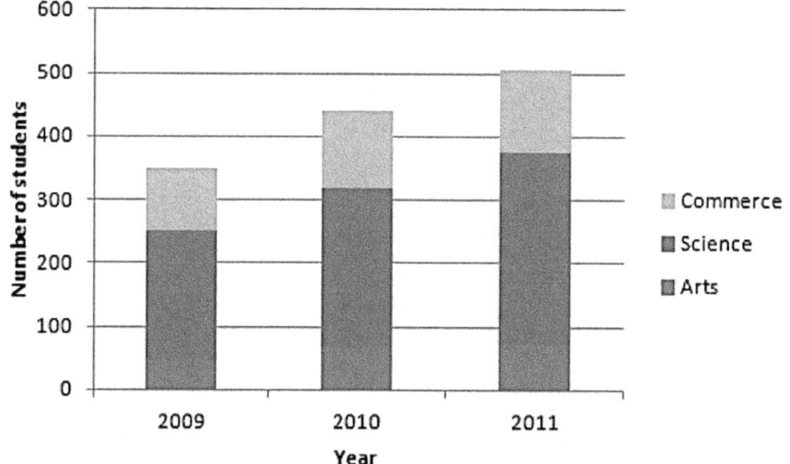

- **Percentage bar diagram:** They are those diagrams which show simultaneously different parts off the values of a sets of data in terms of percentage.

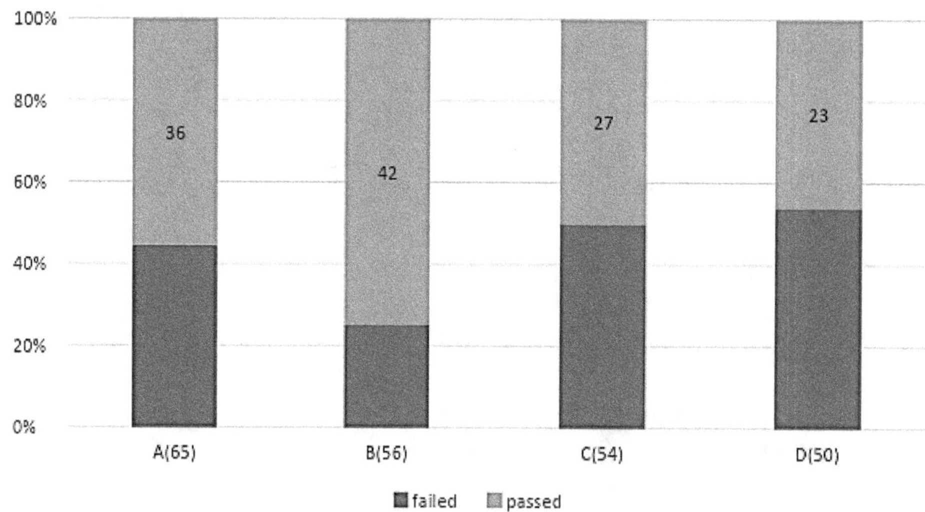

- **Deviation bar diagram:** These are used to compare the net deviation of related variables with respect to time and location. Bars which represent positive deviation and which represent negative deviation are drawn above and below the base line respectively.

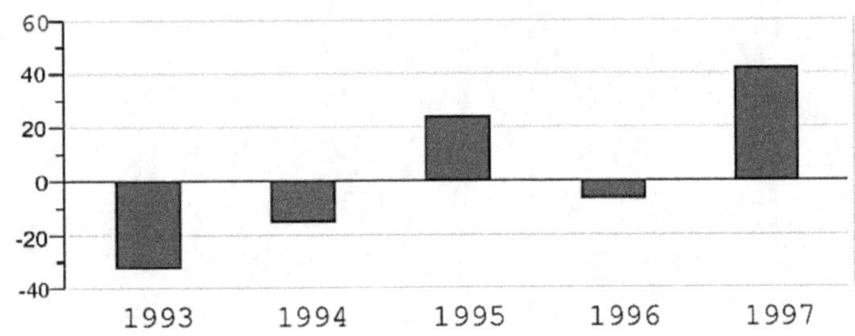

- **Pie Diagram:** Pie or circular diagram is a circle divided into various segments showing the per cent values of a series.

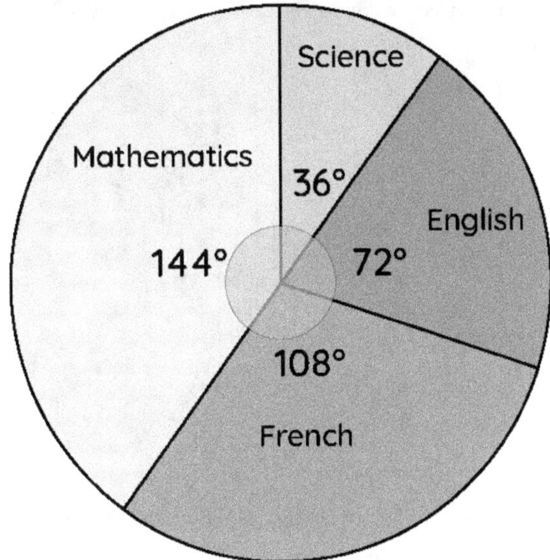

- **Histogram:** Histogram is graphical presentations of a frequency distribution of a continuous series.It can never be drawn for a discrete series.

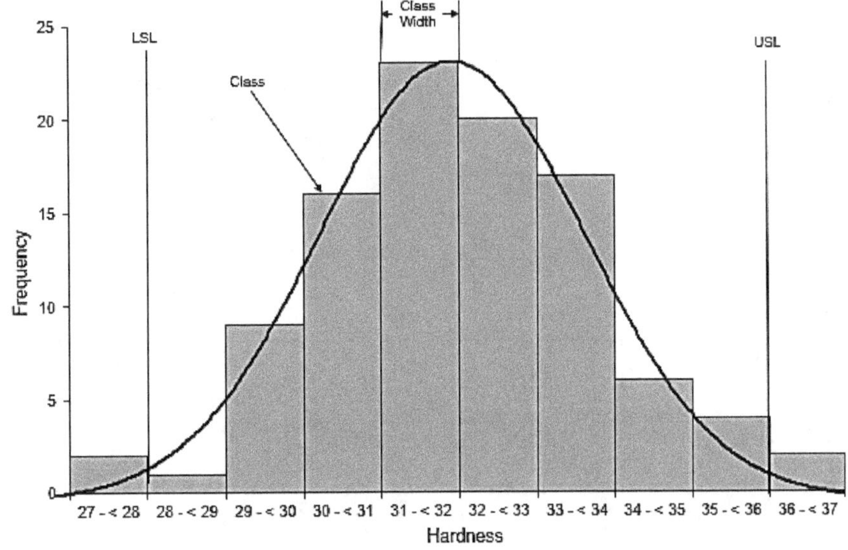

- **Frequency polygon:** Frequency polygon is drawn by joining the mid points of the tops of rectangles in a histogram. It is constructed with the help of discrete as well as continuous series.

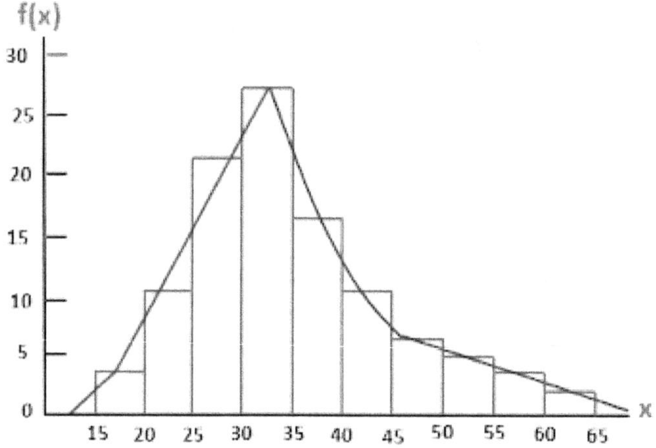

- **Frequency curves:** Cumulative frequency curves or ogive curve is the curve which is constructed by plotting cumulative frequency data on the graph paper in the form of a smooth curve.

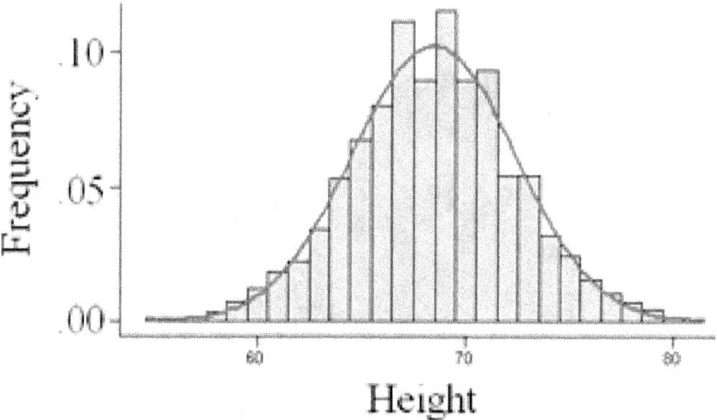

- **Arithmetic line Graphs or Time Series Graphs:** In this graph, time (hour,day, date, week, month, year) is plotted along X-axis and the corresponding value of variable along Y-axis.

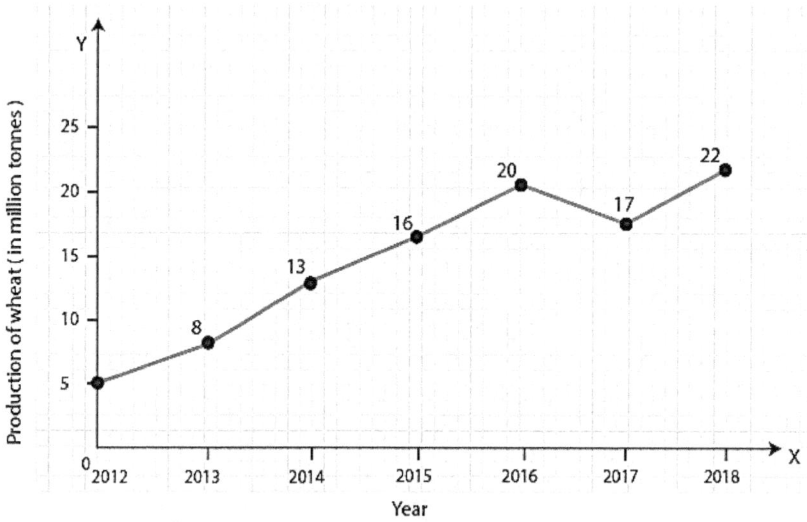

Production of wheat

Multiple Choice Questions

1. The most commonly used device of presenting business and economic data is:

    A. Bar diagrams   **B.** Pictograms

    C. Pie diagrams   **D.** Line diagrams

Answer: A

Explanation:

Bar diagrams are very simple to understand and most suitable for presenting year wise data of sales, profits, etc of the business.

2. With the help of histogram, we can draw:

    A. frequency polygon   **B.** frequency curve

    C. frequency distribution   **D.** All of these

Answer: D

Explanation:

Frequently distribution can be framed from histogram. Frequency polygon and frequency curve can be prepared by converting the mid points of histogram.

3. Frequency curve:

    A. Begins at the origin   **B.** Begins at the horizontal line.

    C. Begins and ends at the base line.   **D.** Passes through the origin

Answer: C

Explanation:

Frequency curve is also called as 'smoothed frequency curve'. The frequency curve also begins and ends in base line (X axis).

4. A pie diagram is also called:

    A. Bar diagram   **B.** Pictogram 12

    C. Line diagram   **D.** Angular diagram

Answer: D

Explanation:

Pie diagrams can be prepared by converting frequencies into angles in such a way that total of all angles should come equal to 360.

5. In volume diagram the three dimensions which are taken into account are:

    A. Length, weight, height   **B.** Length, height, breadth

    C. Length, weight, breadth   **D.** Height, weight, breadth

Answer: B

Explanation:

In volume diagram the three dimensions which are taken into account are Length, height, breadth.

6. Caption stands for:

    A. The column headings   **B.** A numerical information

    C. The row headings   **D.** The table headings

Answer: A

Explanation:

At the top of each column in a table a column designation is given to explain figures of the column. This is called caption.

7. A pictograms is:

    A. A way of measuring the impact of data   **B.** A line drawing

    C. A pictograph   **D.** An illustration where each bar is replaced by a pictures

Answer: D

Explanation:

A pictograms is a graph that shows numerical information by using picture symbols or icon to represent data sets. The advantage of using a pictograph is that it is easy to read.

8. A good title should have following features except:

    A. Placed centrally.   **B.** Brief

    C. Ambiguous   **D.** Clear words

Answer: C

Explanation:

Ambiguous titles may lead to wrong understanding or different understanding of title by the users.

9. A graphical representation of frequency distribution is called a:
   - **A.** Histogram
   - **B.** Time series graph
   - **C.** Frequency
   - **D.** Scatter diagram

Answer: A

Explanation:

Histogram is one of the tools of presentation of data. Other options are not used to present data.

10. The first step in the execution of the inquiry is ________.
    - **A.** processing and analyzing of data.
    - **B.** supervision of field works.
    - **C.** training of field investigators.
    - **D.** setting up of administrative team.

Answer: D

Explanation:

For an enquiry to be made, it is required to set up a team who would do the investigation process, i.e., who would conduct a survey.

11. ______is arranging or organising similar things into groups or classes.
    - **A.** Organising
    - **B.** Classification
    - **C.** Presentation
    - **D.** None of the above

Answer: B

Explanation:

Classification is a process related to categorization in which ideas and objects are recognised, differentiated and understood. It is also a process of identifying a set of categories to which a new observation belongs on the basis of characteristics of a set of data. Hence, classification is arranging or organizing similar things into groups or classes.

12. The purpose of classifying raw data is to ________.
    - **A.** bring order in them
    - **B.** subject them to further statistical analysis easily
    - **C.** Both A and B
    - **D.** None of the above

Answer: C

Explanation:

The purpose of classifying raw data is to bring order in them and subject them to further statistical analysis easily.

13. F-distribution is ________.
    - **A.** Calculated in such a way that the larger variance is always in the numerator.
    - **B.** Equal to the degrees of freedom and variance of distribution
    - **C.** The ratio of sample variances of two normal distributions
    - **D.** Both A and C

Answer: D

Explanation:

F-Distribution is used for the analysis of variance. It is the ratio of sample variances of two normal distributions and its calculated in such a way that the larger variance is always in the numerator.

14. In case of frequency distribution with classes of unequal widths, the heights of bar of a histogram are proportional to ________.
    - **A.** Frequency
    - **B.** Class intervals
    - **C.** Frequency densities
    - **D.** Frequencies in percentage

Answer: C

Explanation:

In Histogram if the classes of unequal width, then the heights of the rectangles must be proportional to the frequency densities.

15. When labels or names are used to identify attributes of elements, it is known as ________.
    - **A.** Quantitative data
    - **B.** Qualitative data
    - **C.** Simple data
    - **D.** None of the above

Answer: B

Explanation:

When labels or names are used to identify attributes of elements, it is known as Qualitative data.

16. _________ means exhibition of data in such a clear and attractive manner that these are easily understood and analyzed.

- **A.** Presentation of data
- **B.** Interpretation of data
- **C.** Collection of data
- **D.** Analysis of data

Answer: A

Explanation:

Presentation of data involves presenting raw facts and figures in the form of tables, charts and diagrams which is easy to understand for the users of data.

17. _________ stands for brief and self-explanatory headings of horizontal rows.

- **A.** Column
- **B.** Caption
- **C.** Stubs
- **D.** None

Answer: C

Explanation:

Like a caption or column heading, each row of the table has to be given a heading. The designations of the rows are also called stubs or stub items, and the complete left column is known as stub column. A brief description of the row headings may also be given at the left-hand top in the table.

18. Diagrams which take shapes like rectangles, squares, circles, cubes, sphere etc. are called:

- **A.** Pictographs
- **B.** Line graphs
- **C.** Geometric graphs
- **D.** None

Answer: C

Explanation:

Examples of geometric graphs are bar diagrams, pie diagrams, etc.

19. Percentage bar diagram has:

- **A.** equal width and equal interval
- **B.** data expressed in percentages.
- **C.** equal width
- **D.** equal interval

Answer: B

Explanation:

For contacting a percentage bar graph, data has to be converted in percentage form. Percentage bar diagrams have the same length.

20. Which of the following is not rule for constructing a line graph:

- **A.** Both Y-scale and X-scale must be labeled
- **B.** Equal magnitude must be represented by equal distances.
- **C.** Y scale must begin at one as origin similarly Y-scale
- **D.** None

Answer: C

Explanation:

An arithmetic line graph is also called time series graph. In this graph time (hour, day/date, week, month, year, etc.) is plotted along X-axis and the value of the variable (time series data) along Y-axis. A line graph by joining these plotted points, thus, obtained is called arithmetic line graph (time series graph). It helps in understanding the trend, periodicity, etc. in a long term time series data.

21. The width of a class interval in a frequency distribution (or bar chart) will be approximately equal to the range of the data divided by the __________.

- **A.** Total of frequency
- **B.** Number of class intervals
- **C.** Highest value in data
- **D.** Lowest value in data set

Answer: B

Explanation:

For example, if the data is about marks of students in a 100 marks paper, and data is presented in the form of marks 0-10, 10-20, 20-30 etc. The range of the data will be 100-0=100. The number of class intervals is 10. Therefore, width of the class intervals will be 100/10=10.

22. Ogives for more than type and less than type distribution intersect at:

- **A.** Mean
- **B.** Median
- **C.** Mode
- **D.** Origin

Answer: B

Explanation:

Mean and mode cannot be calculated by using graphical method. Only median can be ascertained by constructing ogives.

23. ____ refers to the method or process of presenting data in the form of rows and columns and ____ refers to the actual presentation of data on the form of rows and columns.

    A. Graph, Table   **B.** Tabulation, Table

    C. Table, Tabulation   **D.** Tabulation, Graph

Answer: B

Explanation:

In a tabular presentation, data are presented in rows (read horizontally) and columns (read vertically). The most simple way of conceptualising a table is to present the data in rows and columns alongwith some explanatory notes. Tabulation can be done using one-way, two-way or three-way classification depending upon the number of characteristics involved.

24. If the upper limits of the classes and proceed by adding the frequencies this method will be called:

    A. More than type ogive   **B.** Less than type ogive

    C. Both   **D.** None

Answer: B

Explanation:

For "less than" ogive the cumulative frequencies are plotted against the respective upper limits of the class intervals.

25. A ______ becomes a ____ if we draw a line joining mid-points of the tops of all rectangles.

    A. Histogram, Frequency Polygon   **B.** Histogram, Frequency

    C. Histogram, Frequency Curve   **D.** Histogram, Frequency distribution

Answer: A

Explanation:

A frequency polygon is a plane bounded by straight lines, usually four or more lines. Frequency polygon is an alternative to histogram and is also derived from histogram itself. A frequency polygon can be fitted to a histogram for studying the shape of the curve. The simplest method of drawing a frequency polygon is to join the midpoints of the topside of the consecutive rectangles of the histogram.

26. In a cumulative percent frequency distribution, the last class will have a cumulative percent frequency equal to:

    A. 100   **B.** Zero

    C. -1   **D.** 100%

Answer: D

Explanation:

In a cumulative percent frequency distribution, the last class will have a cumulative percent frequency equal to 100%.

27. A tabular summary of a set of data, which shows the frequency of the appearance of data elements in several no overlapping classes is termed:

    A. a frequency distribution   **B.** a histogram

    C. a frequency polygon   **D.** the class width

Answer: A

Explanation:

A frequency distribution is defined as an orderly arrangement of data classified according to the magnitude of the observations.

28. When data are classified according to a single characteristic, it is called:

    A. Quantitative classification   **B.** Qualitative classification

    C. Simple classification   **D.** Area classification

Answer: C

Explanation:

If we classify the data concerning a single characteristic, then this is recognized as a one-way classification.

29. Which of the following graphs should be used to represent the percentage of boys and girls in a class?

    A. Bar graph   **B.** Pie chart

    C. Line graph   **D.** Venn diagram

Answer: B

Explanation:

Pie chart.

It is a type of graph in which a circle is divided into sectors such that each represents a proportion of the whole. Percentage is usually represented with the help of these sectors.

30. If the monthly expenditure pattern of a person who earns a monthly salary of Rs. 15,000 is represented in a pie graph, then the sector angle of an item on transport expenses measures 15°. What is his monthly expenditure on transport?

    A. Rs. 450   **B.** Rs. 625

    C. Rs. 675   **D.** Cannot be computed from the given data.

Answer: B

Explanation:

Using the formula for area of a sector, monthly expenditure on transport $= \dfrac{15°}{360} \times$ Rs. 1500 = Rs. 625

Chapter – 5   Statistical Tools and Interpretation

Introduction

Statistical tools play a critical role in analyzing data related to economic activities such as production, consumption, distribution, banking, insurance, trade, and transport. This chapter emphasizes the use of statistical tools and methods in diverse types of analyses to develop a project. Conducting surveys, collecting data from consumers, analyzing the implementation of technology in schools, and creating reports are some examples of how statistical tools can be applied. The primary objective is to gather pertinent information and recommend enhancements to products or systems.

Measures of Central Tendency

Measures of central tendency help in understanding data in a summarized way by identifying a central point of data. It basically means finding that central location, around which the data is clustered. Most commonly used measures of central tendency are mean, median, mode.

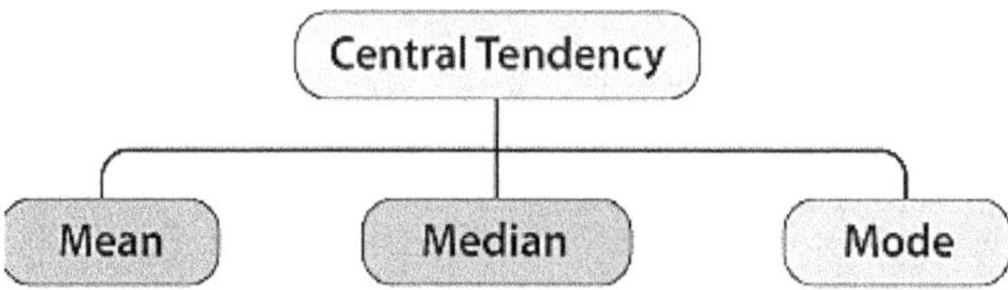

Mean

The mean is a measure of central tendency of the data and is also called the average of the numbers. The mean is found by adding all the numbers and dividing that by a number of values in the data set.

$$x_1 + x_2 + x_3 + \cdots \ldots + x_n/n$$

For eg: Strength of IIM Ahmedabad is 300, the strength of IIM Bangalore is 400, the strength of IIM Calcutta is 200 and strength of IIM Shillong is 100, you need to find the mean of the strength of all the four IIM's.

You will start by adding all the numbers in the given data = 300+400+200+100= 1000
Post that you need to divide this number by the number of values i.e., 250.
Hence, 1000/4= 250

Mean of all the four IIM's combined is 250.
This is the most basic concept behind finding mean but most important as well. If you understand what is being done, no matter how tricky the question might be, you just need to remember the core concept.

Median

Median is defined as the middle value of the set. In order to find the median of a data set, you need to first arrange that set in ascending order and then:
* If the no. of values is odd- you just pick the middle value and that is your median.
* If the no. of values is even- find the average of middle two numbers and your median will be the answer you get.

Mode

Mode is the easiest measure of central tendency to calculate. It is the number that occurs the most number of times in a data set.
For eg: 2,3,4,2,5,2,2,2,5,9
The mode in the above data set will be 2 as it is the only number which has appeared 5 times in the above data set.

Measures of Dispersion – Statistical Tools and Interpretation

When the values in a data set are large, the data set usually tends to scatter. Dispersion is basically used to measure the variation of an item and to see how to spread out a data set.
Here are the methods for measuring dispersion:
* Range

- Quartile Deviation
- Standard Deviation
- Mean Deviation

Range

Range of a data set is calculated by finding out the difference between the highest value and the lowest value of the data set.

Quartile Deviation

- Inter Quartile Range= Q3-Q1 (symbol Q represent quartile in the series)
- Quartile deviation is defined as the semi-interquartile range i.e., Q3 – Q1 / 2

Standard Deviation

A standard deviation is a statistical tool which measures the dispersion in a data set in respect to its mean and is calculated as the square root of the squares of items from the mean values.

Mean deviation

The mean deviation is defined as a statistical measure that is used to calculate the average deviation from the mean value of the given data set.

Calculate Standard Deviation

Direct Method

Standard deviation is calculated by dividing the sum total of the squares of deviation with the number of items and then finding its square root.

$$\sigma = \sqrt{\Sigma X^2 / N}$$

Short-cut method:

$$\sigma = \sqrt{[(\Sigma D^2/N) - (\Sigma D/N)^2]}$$

This method assumes any random value for deviation.

Step deviation Method-

$$\sigma = \sqrt{[(\Sigma D'^2/N) - (\Sigma D'/N)^2]} \times C$$

This method selects a common factor among deviations so that when deviations get divided by this factor, deviation gets reduced, thus making the calculation simpler.

Correlation – Statistical tools and interpretation

Correlation is a statistical tool which studies the relationship between two variables e.g. change in price leads to change in quantity demanded.

Correlation studies and measures the direction and intensity of relationship among variables. It measures co-variation not causation. It does not imply cause and effect relation.

Types of correlation

- **Negative correlation:** Eg: price and demand of a product
- **Positive correlation:** Eg: price and supply of a product

Properties of correlation coefficient(r)

- Correlation coefficient (r) has no unit.
- A negative value of r indicates an inverse relation.
- If r is positive then two variables move in the same direction.
- The value of r lies between minus – 1 and +1, i.e.,
- If r is zero, the two variables are uncorrelated.
- If r = + 1 or r = – 1, the correlation is perfect.
- A high value of r indicates strong linear relationship and a low value or indicates a weak linear relationship.
- The value of r is unaffected by the change of origin and change of scale.

Methods to Calculate Correlation

1. Scatter diagram
2. Karl person's coefficient of correlation.
3. Spearman's rank correlation.

1. Scatter diagram

Scatter diagram offers a graphic expression of the direction and degree of correlation. To construct a scatter diagram, x variables taken on X-axis and y variable is taken on Y-axis. The cluster of points, plotted is referred to as a scatter diagram. In this, the degree of closeness of scatter points and their overall direction enables us to examine the relationship.

2. Karl person's coefficient of correlation

Karl person's coefficient of correlation is a quantitative method of calculating correlation. It gives a precise numerical value of the degree of linear relationship between two variables. Karl person's coefficient of correlation is also known as product moment correlation.

Formula:

$$r = \frac{\Sigma xy}{N\sigma \times \sigma y}$$

Here,

r	=	Coefficient of correlation
x	=	$(X - \overline{X})$
y	=	$(Y - Y)$
σx	=	Standard deviation of X − series
σy	=	Standard deviation of Y − serise
N	=	Number of observations

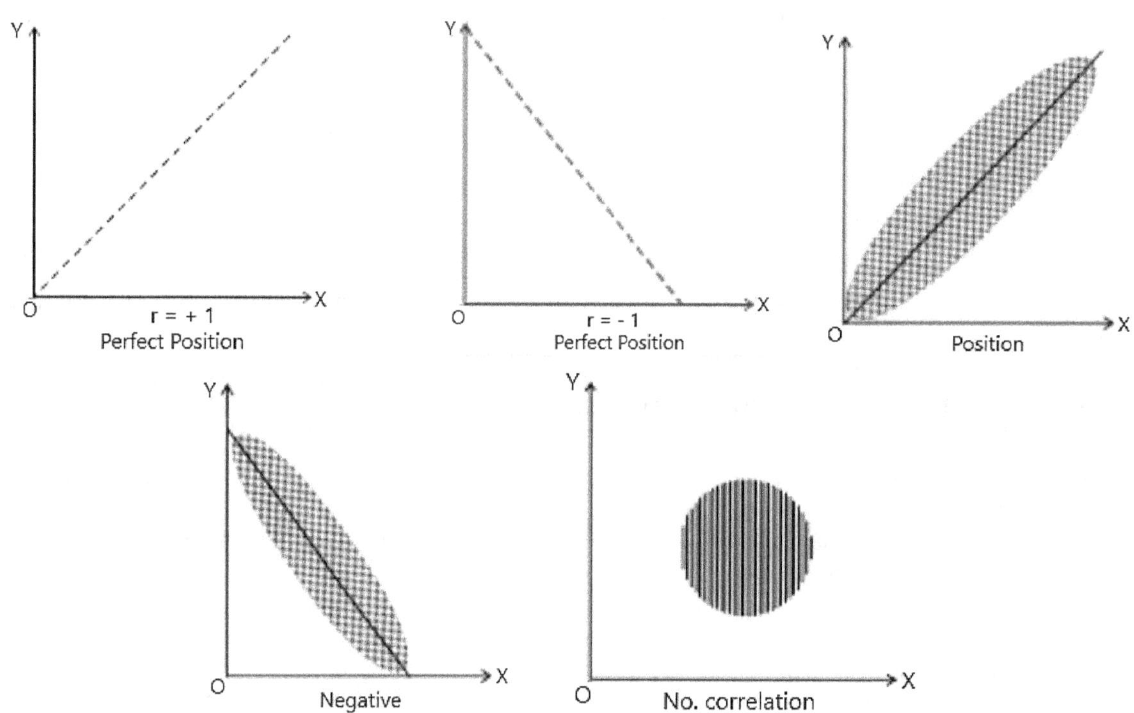

Karl Person's coefficient of correlation is calculated by following methods:

$$r = \frac{\Sigma xy}{\sqrt{\Sigma x^2 \cdot \Sigma y^2}}$$

- **Actual mean method:**

Here, r = Coeff. Of correlation

$$x = (X - \bar{X})$$
$$y = (Y - Y$$

- **Assumed Mean method:**

$$r = \frac{\sum XY - \frac{\sum X \sum Y}{N}}{\sqrt{\left(\sum X^2 - \frac{(\sum X)^2}{N}\right)\left(\sum Y^2 - \frac{(\sum Y)^2}{N}\right)}}$$

$$r = \frac{N\Sigma dx \cdot dy - (\Sigma dx)(\Sigma dy)}{\sqrt{N\Sigma dx^2 - (\Sigma dx)^2}\sqrt{N\Sigma dy^2 - (\Sigma dy)^2}}$$

Here,

dx = Deviations of X-series from assumec

dy = Deviation of Y-series from assumed

$\sum dxdy$ = Sum of multiple of dx and dy.

$\sum dx^2$ = Sum of the square of dx.

$\sum dy^2$ = Sum of the square of dy.

$\sum dx$ = Sum of the deviation of X-series.

$\sum dy$ = Sum of the deviation of Y-series.

N = Number of pairs of observations

When value of the variables are large, we use step deviation method to reduce the burden of calculation.

- **Step deviation method:**

$$r = \frac{\Sigma dx'dy' - \frac{\Sigma dx' \times \Sigma dy'}{n}}{\sqrt{\Sigma dx'^2 - \frac{(\Sigma dx')^2}{n}} \times \sqrt{\Sigma dy'^2 - \frac{(\Sigma dy')^2}{n}}}$$

Here, $dx' = \frac{dx}{C_1}$

$dx = \frac{dy}{C_2}$

dx = deviation of X-series from assumed mean = $(X - A)$

dy = deviation of Y-series from assumed mean = $(Y - A)$

$\sum dxdy$ = Sum of multiple of dx and dy.

$\sum dx^2$ = Sum of the square of dx.

$\sum dy^2$ = Sum of the square of dy.

$\sum dx$ = Sum of the deviation of x-series.

$\sum dy$ = Sum of the deviation of Y-series.

N = Number of pairs of observations

C_1 is common factor for series $-x$

C_2 is common factor for series $-y$

3. Spearman's rank correlation

Spearman's rank correlation method is used to calculate coefficient of correlation of qualitative variables such as beauty, bravery, wisdom, ability virtue etc. It was developed by British Psychologist C.E. spearman.

Formula $r_s = 1 - \frac{6\Sigma D^2}{N^3 - N}$

Here,

r_s = Coefficient of rank correlation.

D = Rank differences

N = Numbers of rank

When ranks are repeated the formula is:

$$r_s = 1 - \frac{6\left[\Sigma d^2 + \frac{(m_1^3 - m_1)}{12} + \frac{(m_2^3 - m_2)}{12} + \cdots \cdots\right]}{N^3 - N}$$

Where $m_1, m_2 \ldots \ldots \ldots \ldots i$ are number of repetitions of ranks.

Index numbers are a statistical tool which helps in measuring variations between the related variables of a group. They act as a relative measure of a group of data, and they offer a precise measurement of the quantitative change in the concerned variables.

Index numbers help in understanding the changes in standard of living and acts as a barometer for measuring money as well. Index numbers are also really helpful in major decisions related to businesses such as determining the rate of the premium.

Features of Index Number
- Index numbers are expressed in terms of percentages. However, percentage sign (%) is never used.
- Index numbers are relative measurement of group of data.
- Index numbers offer a precise measurement of the quantitative change in the concerned variables over time.
- Index number show changes in terms of averages.
- They are expressed in numbers.
- Index number facilitates the comparative study over different time period.

Importance of Index number
- It serves as a barometer for measuring the value of money.
- Gives knowledge about change in standard of living.
- It helps the business community in planning their decision.
- Helpful to determine the rate of premium.

Limitation of Index Number
- Limited applicability
- International comparison is not possible
- Limited coverage
- Difficulty in the construction of index number

Types of Index numbers
- Wholesale price index (WPI)
- Consumer price index (CPI) or Cost of living index
- Index of industrial production (IIP)
- Index of Agricultural production (IAP)

Wholesale price index (WPI)
The Wholesale Price Index represents the price of a basket of wholesale goods. WPI focuses on the price of goods that are traded between corporations. It does not concentrate on goods purchased by the consumers.
- The main objective of WPI is monitoring price drifts that reflect demand and supply in manufacturing, construction and industry.
- WPI helps in assessing the macroeconomic as well as microeconomic conditions of an economy.

Importance of WPI
- In a dynamic world, prices do not remain constant.
- The inflation rate calculated on the basis of the movement of the Wholesale Price Index (WPI) is an important measure to monitor the dynamic movement of prices.
- As WPI captures price movements in a most comprehensive way, it is widely used by Government, banks, industry and business circles.
- Significant monetary and fiscal policy changes are often linked to WPI movements.
- Similarly, the movement of WPI serves as an influential determinant, in the formulation of trade, fiscal and other economic policies by the Government of India.
- The WPI indices are also used for the purpose of escalation clauses in the supply of raw materials, machinery and construction work.
- WPI is used as a deflator of various nominal macroeconomic variables, including Gross Domestic Product (GDP).

Consumer price index (CPI) or Cost of living index
Consumer price index is referred to as that index that is used in calculating the retail inflation in the economy by tracking the changes in prices of most commonly used goods and services.

In other words, the consumer price index calculates the changes in price of a common basket of goods and services. It is also called a market basket and is used for calculating the price variations in fixed items.

- The market basket that is used by CPI in calculating price changes represents the most common goods and services that are consumed within the economy and is therefore the weighted average for those goods and services.
- The items that are considered as a basket are goods related to food, clothing, transportation, housing, electronics, apparels, education, medicine, etc.
- CPI can be used to calculate the cost of living of the people of a country and also the changes in the purchasing power of the currency of a nation.
- CPI detects the price changes of the items falling under the common basket and by averaging those prices.
- CPI is found to be a good measure for determining the rise in prices (also referred to as inflation) and falling prices (referred to as deflation).

Importance of CPI

CPI is a widely used measure for determining inflation in an economy. Rising inflation results in the diminishing standard of living for the residents of a nation. Over a period of time, it will result in an increase in the cost of living.

A high inflation rate will result in increase in prices of goods and as a result there will be less manufacturing, which will result in loss of jobs.

Index of industrial production (IIP)

The Index of Industrial Production (IIP) is a composite indicator that compares the volume of production of a basket of industrial products during a particular period to that of a base period.

Characteristics of Index of Industrial Production

- IIP is a composite indicator that gauges the pace of growth of many industry categories.
- Mining, manufacturing and electricity industries are all broad sectors.
- Use based sectors, such as Basic Goods, Capital Goods, and Intermediate Goods.
- It includes eight core industries of India representing 40% of the weight of items that are included in the IIP.
- Eight Core Sectors/Industries included in IIP are electricity (19.85%), steel (17.92%), refinery products (28.04%), crude oil (8.98%), coal (10.33%), cement (5.37%), natural gas (6.88%), fertilizers (2.63%).

Importance of Index of Industrial Production

- It is used to measure the physical volume of production.
- It is used by different government agencies for various policy-making initiatives such as the Ministry of Finance, the Reserve Bank of India, etc.
- It is also used for the calculation of the quarterly and advance GDP estimates.
- This index is also used by business analysts, financial experts, and the private industry for different purposes.
- It also tells about the Gross Value Added of the manufacturing sector quarterly.

Methods of constructing index numbers

1. **Construction of Simple Index numbers**
- Simple Aggregative Method

$$P_{01} = \frac{\Sigma P_1}{\Sigma P_0} \times 100$$

Here, P_{01} = Price index of the current year.
ΣP_1 = Sum of the prices of the commodities in the current year
ΣP_0 = Sum of the prices of the commodities in the base year

Current year: Current year is the year for which average change is to be measured or index of index number is to be calculated.
Base year: Base year is the year of reference from which we want measure extent of change in the current year. The index number of base year is generally assumed to be 100.

- Simple Average of Price Relatives Method

$$P_{01} = \frac{\Sigma \left(\frac{P_1}{P_0} \times 100 \right)}{N}$$

Here, P_{01} = Price index of the current year

$\frac{P_1}{P_0} \times 100$ = Price relatives

N = Number of commodities

2. **Construction of weighted Index numbers**
- Weighted Average of Price Relative Method

$$P_{01} = \frac{\Sigma RW}{\Sigma W}$$

Here, P_{01} = Index number for the current year in relation to base year

W = Weight,

R = Price relatives i.e. $\frac{P_1}{P_0} \times 100$

- Weighted Aggregative Method

(i) Laspeyre's method: $P_{01} = \frac{\Sigma p_1 q_0}{\Sigma p_0 q_0} \times 100$

(ii) Pasche's method: $P_{01} = \frac{\Sigma p_1 q_1}{\Sigma p_0 q_1} \times 100$

(iii) Fisher's Method: $P_{01} = \sqrt{\frac{\Sigma p_1 q_0}{\Sigma p_0 q_0} \times \frac{\Sigma p_1 q_1}{\Sigma p_0 q_1}} \times 100$

Index of Agricultural production (IAP)

While discussing geographical types of agriculture, Enyedi (1964) devised technique (8) for determining an index of productivity coefficient.

Enyedi's formula of productivity index is:

Productivity Index, $PI = \frac{Y}{Yn} \div \frac{T}{Tn}$

Where
- Y is the total production of the selected crop in unit area,
- Yn is the total production of the same crop on a national scale,
- T is the total cropped area of the unit area, and
- Tn is the total cropped area on a national scale.

Multiple Choice Questions

1. ___________ is the most frequently observed data value.
   - **A.** Arithmetic Mean
   - **C.** Median

   B. Mode

   D. All of the above

   Answer: B

   Explanation:

   The mode is the most frequently observed data value.

2. Mode of 2, 3, 4, 5, 0, 1, 3, 3, 4, 3 is ____________.
   - **A.** 3
   - **C.** 2

   B. 5

   D. 1

   Answer: A

   Explanation:

   Mode is the term which appears maximum number of times.

   The terms are: 2, 3, 4, 5, 0, 1, 3, 3, 4, 3

   Arranging them in ascending order: 0,1,2,3,3,3,3,4,4,5

   3 is occurring maximum number of times. hence mode is 3.

3. Median is _________ the Arithmetic Mean and Mode.
   - **A.** Always between
   - **C.** Always less than

   B. Always greater than

   D. None of the above

   Answer: A

   Explanation:

The arithmetic mean is found by adding the numbers and dividing the sum by the number of numbers in the list. This is what is most often meant by an average. The median is the middle value in a list ordered from smallest to largest. The mode is the most frequently occurring value on the list.

4. _________ is used to describe Qualitative data.
   A. Mean
   C. Median
   B. Mode
   D. None

Answer: B

Explanation:
Mode of a statistical data is the variate which has maximum frequency and only mode can be used for qualitative data.

5. The algebraic sum of deviation of a set of n values from Mean is ___________.
   A. n
   C. 0
   B. 1
   D. None

Answer: C

Explanation:
The algebraic sum of the deviations of a set of n values from its arithmetic mean is zero.

6. For mode in continuous series, class intervals _______ be equal and series _______ be exclusive.
   A. Should, can
   C. Should, should
   B. Can, should
   D. Can, can

Answer: C

Explanation:
For mode in a continuous series, the class intervals should be equal, and the series should be exclusive.

7. Mode of data 1,1,2,2,5,3,4,4 is _____________.
   A. 1,2,5
   C. 2,3,5
   B. 1,2,4
   D. 3,4,5

Answer: B

Explanation:
The mode of a set of data refers to the value that appears most frequently. In the given data set of 1, 1, 2, 2, 5, 3, 4, 4, the mode is 1, 2, 4 because it repeated twice, which is more frequently than any other value in the set.

8. The most commonly used measure of central tendency is______.
   A. AM
   C. Mode
   B. Media
   D. GM and HM

Answer: D

Explanation:
Arithmetic mean refers to the average amount in a given group of data. It is defined as the summation of all the observation is the data which is divided by the number of observations in the data. It is the most commonly used measure of central tendency because it includes all the observation in a given data and in comparison to other measures of central tendency, arithmetic mean has very simple application.

9. Arithmetic Mean is equal to _______________.
   A. Sum of values of observations / No: of observations
   C. Sum of values of observations + No: of observations
   B. Half of values of observations x No: of observations
   D. Sum of values of observations % No: of observations

Answer: A

Explanation:
The mean (or average) of a number of observations is the sum of the values of all the observations divided by the total number of observations.
Arithmetic Mean = Sum of values of observations / No: of observations.

10. ______ is the positioned value of the variable which divides the distribution into two equal parts.
   A. Mean
   C. Mode
   B. Median
   D. None

Answer: B

Explanation:

The median is the middle value of a variable of a distribution which divides it into two equal parts. It is the value of the variable such that the number of observations above it is equal to the number of observations below it.

11. Median of the following numbers: 4, 4, 5, 7, 6, 7, 7, 12, 3 is:

    A. 5   **B.** 4

    C. 6   **D.** 2

Answer: C

Explanation:

Terms are: 4, 4, 5, 7, 6, 7, 7, 12, 3.

Arranging the terms in ascending order: 3, 4, 4, 5, 6, 7, 7, 7, 12.

Since the number of terms is odd the median will be the middle term i.e. 5th term which is 6.

12. The difference of median and mode of the following data 25, 33, 72, 65, 29, 60, 30, 54, 32, 53, 42, 52, 51, 42, 48, 45, 47, 46, 33 is:

    A. 3.5   **B.** 5.4

    C. 1.5   **D.** 6.5

Answer: A

Explanation:

Ascending order of the following data, 25, 29, 30, 32, 33, 33, 42, 42, 42, 45, 46, 47, 48, 51, 52, 53, 54, 60, 65, 72

Total number of values = 20

10th data = 45 and 11th data = 46

$\Rightarrow$ Median = (45 + 46)/2 = 45.5

42 occurred 3 times

$\Rightarrow$ Mode of the following data = 42

$\therefore$ The difference of median and mode of the following data = (45.5 – 42) = 3.5

13. ________ is the middle element when the data is arranged in the order of magnitude.

    A. Mean   **B.** Mode

    C. Median   **D.** Integrity

Answer: C

Explanation:

The median of a given data set or observations is the middle-most value after arranging the data in an ascending or a descending order.

14. ________ concentrates on central items of data.

    A. Mean   **B.** Median

    C. Integral   **D.** Both A and C

Answer: B

Explanation:

Median concentrates on central items of data. The median is the middle value. It is the value that splits the dataset in half, making it a natural measure of central tendency.

15. ________ are the measures which divides the data into four equal parts?

    A. Mono   **B.** BI-parties

    C. Quartiles   **D.** None

Answer: C

Explanation:

The quartile is defined as the middle number between the smallest number and the median of the data set. They are those values which divide the total set of data into four equal parts.

16. __________ divides the distribution into 100 equal parts.

    A. Quartile   **B.** Percentile

    C. Median   **D.** All of the above

Answer: B

Explanation:

A percentile (or a centile) is a measure used in statistics indicating the value below which a given percentage of observations in a group of observations fall.

For example, the 20th percentile is the value (or score) below which 20 percent of the observations may be found.

The term percentile and the related term percentile rank are often used in the reporting of scores from norm-referenced tests.

For example, if a score is in the 86th percentile, it is higher than 86% of the other scores.
100th percentile being the maximum, it therefore divides the items into 100 equal parts.

17. _______ is the median value in percentile.
- **A.** p_{100}
- **B.** p_{50}
- **C.** p_{75}
- **D.** p_{25}

Answer: B

Explanation:

The 25th percentile is also known as the first quartile (Q_1), the 50th percentile as the median or second quartile (Q_2), and the 75th percentile as the third quartile (Q_3).

18. Calculate Mean of 40, 50, 55, 78, 58.
- **A.** 56.2
- **B.** 65.4
- **C.** 44.0
- **D.** 33.5

Answer: A

Explanation:

Given marks:

$40, 50, 55, 78, 58$

Here, the number of data values = 5

We know that:

Mean = Sum of data values/Total number of data values

$= (40 + 50 + 55 + 78 + 58)/5$

$= 281/5$

$= 56.2$

19. In order to save time in calculating mean from a data set containing a large no: of observations we use _________.
- **A.** Direct method
- **B.** Assumed Mean
- **C.** Both A and B
- **D.** None of these

Answer: B

Explanation:

In order to save time in calculating mean from a data set containing a large no: of observations we use Assumed Mean.

20. Which Quartile is called Median?
- **A.** Q_0
- **B.** Q_1
- **C.** Q_2
- **D.** None

Answer: C

Explanation:

The median is considered the second quartile (Q_2). The interquartile range is the difference between upper and lower quartiles. The semi-interquartile range is half the interquartile range.

Chapter – 1 Introduction

Microeconomics is a branch of economics studying the behavior of an individual economic unit. Adam Smith is known as the father of economics and microeconomics. Microeconomics help in contemplating the attributes of different decision-makers in an economy like individuals, enterprises, and households. In simple terms, microeconomics help in understanding why and how different goods have different values, how individuals make certain decisions, and how do they cooperate with each other.

Economy

The word 'economy' was taken from a french word, 'economie'. It is a system in which people earn their livelihoods and live through production, consumption, investment and exchange to satisfy their wants and needs.

An economy is a broad collection of interconnected production, consumption, and trade activities that aid in distributing scarce resources. Goods and services are produced, consumed, and distributed to suit the requirements of those who live and work in an economy, also known as an economic system.

Types of Economy

Microeconomics, there are 3 different types of economy:

1. **Capitalist economy or Market economy:** It is a system of the economy where all the materials and means of production are owned and operated by private individuals. This concept of economy or type of economy has only one major aim or motive, which is to earn profits.
2. **Socialist economy or Planned economy:** On the contrary to the capitalist or market economy, the socialist economy is one where the government owns all the means and materials of production. The government is the centrally planned authority of any nation who takes all the important decisions regarding production, exchange, consumption, availability of goods and services, distribution of goods and services, etc. They have the main aim or motive to produce for social welfare.
3. **Mixed economy:** A mixed economy is that type of economy with traits and characteristics of both the above-mentioned economies- capitalist and socialist.

Economic Problem

Economic problem is the problem of choosing from among different options that arise because of three major reasons limited resources, unlimited human wants, and alternative use of the limited resources.

- **Scarcity of resources:** Resources such as capital, land, labor, etc., are limited in an economy as compared to their demand. Therefore, an economy cannot manufacture everything they want which creates an economic problem.
- **Unlimited human wants:** An individual's wants never end, they always want something and can never be satisfied completely. As soon as they accomplish one want, another arises. Their priorities are also different and hence create an economic problem.
- **Alternate uses:** The resources available in the economy are not only scarce, but they also have alternate uses. It means that a resource can be used in different ways, which makes the need to choose among the available resources essential, ultimately giving rise to economic problems.

Positive Economics and Normative Economics

Positive economics is the study of the facts of life. It means that it deals with the real life economic problems as they are and how these problems are solved.

However, normative economics deals with finding out solutions to economic problems. Simply put, it answers the question 'what ought to be done.'

Microeconomics

The term 'micro' in microeconomics is derived from the Greek word 'mikros' meaning 'small.' It was founded by the father of economics, Adam Smith. Microeconomics is the study of the individual units of an economy. It means that in microeconomics, we study the behavior and choices made by individual businesses and consumers with the changes in different aspects of goods and services in an economy. The four major components of microeconomics are consumer behavior, market supply and demand, individual preferences driving producers, and market-specific labor markets. It helps in determining how one can achieve equilibrium at a small scale. For example, consumer equilibrium, individual demand, individual supply, individual savings, price determination of a commodity, etc.

Macroeconomics

The term 'macros' in macroeconomics is derived from the Greek word 'makros' meaning 'large.' Macroeconomics is the study of the economy as a whole. It means that in macroeconomics, we study the behavior and choices made by the whole economy with the changes in different aspects of goods and services in an economy. Hence, its main focus is on the aggregate growth and correlation of an economy. The major components of macroeconomics are unemployment, inflation, and national output. It helps in determining how to achieve equilibrium in the income and employment level of a country. For example, general price level, poverty, rate of unemployment, national income, aggregate supply, aggregate demand, etc.

Central Problems of an Economy

The basic economic activities of life are production, distribution, and disposition of goods and services. A society will be facing scarcity of resources during the time of fulfillment of these activities. Scarcity is evident, due to the availability of limited resources, and human needs having no limit. This variation between the supply and demand leads to the formation of central problems of an economy.

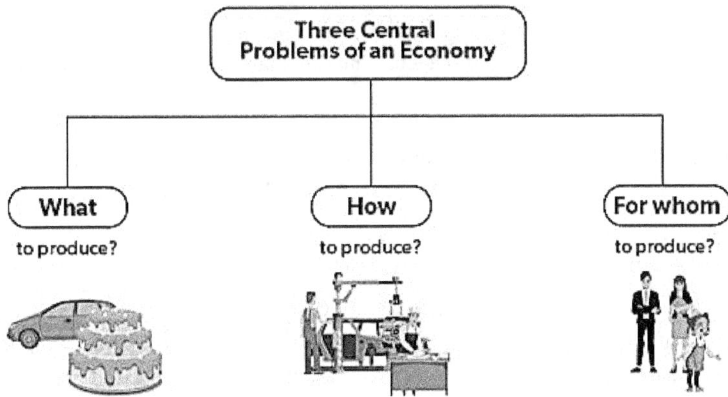

What to produce?
With limited resources, an economy cannot produce all goods and services. It has to choose among the different goods and services. Therefore, the first central problem of an economy includes selecting goods and services to produce and the number of units or quantity of each commodity to be produced. For example, a farmer has to make choice between different crops as to which he should grow on one piece of land. He can decide to grow one crop of the whole land or grow different proportions of more than one crop.

How to produce?
After deciding what to produce, another central problem of how to manufacture the goods and services arises. It involves selecting a technique of production from among different techniques. Usually, there are two techniques of production, labor intensive techniques, and capital-intensive techniques. The former technique involves more use of labor, and the latter involves more use of machines. An organization can decide the technique based on different factors like the nature of the product, size of the market, size of the location, budget, etc. For example, a poor farmer can adopt labor intensive techniques as they are cheap. However, a rich farmer can adopt capital intensive techniques as he can afford to purchase machines.

For whom to produce?
The last central problem of an economy after deciding what and how to produce is for whom to produce. As an economy cannot satisfy the needs and wants of every individual of the society, it has to make a decision for who to produce a commodity and service. Simply put, it involves deciding who should get how much of the goods and services, i.e., how much production should be done for the poor and how much for the rich. For example, an organization can decide to produce necessity goods for the poor section of society. However, another firm can decide to produce luxury goods for the rich section of society.
Besides these problems, there are two more problems that arise in underdeveloped countries like India. These are the problems of the growth of resources and the problem of the underutilization of resources.

Production possibility frontier (PPF) is referred to as a graph that shows the maximum possible output that can be achieved by two goods when the input is maintained constant or fixed. The factors that are included in the input are natural resources, capital goods, Labour and entrepreneurship.

The production of one good can be increased when the production of the other good is sacrificed. The Production Possibility Frontier (PPF) is also known as the Production Possibility Curve. The production possibility frontier represents the concepts of scarcity, tradeoffs and choice and the shape of the curve will change based on whether the price costs are constant, increasing or decreasing.

The slope of the PPF is indicative of the opportunity cost of producing a good in comparison to another good. The same can be used for comparing the opportunity costs of another producer for determining the comparative advantage.

Multiple Choice Questions

1. Which Economist divided Economics in two branches of micro and macro on the basis of economic activity?
    - **A.** Marshall
    - **B.** Ricardo
    - **C.** Ragnar Frisch
    - **D.** None of these

Answer: C

Explanation:
Ragnar Frisch is a Norwegian economist who created the terms 'microeconomics' and 'macroeconomics" for the first time in the year 1993.

2. Which of the following is studied under Microeconomics?
    - **A.** Individual unit
    - **B.** Economic Aggregate
    - **C.** National Income
    - **D.** Factor pricing

Answer: D

Explanation:
Microeconomics deals with the study of economics from the viewpoint of an individual unit. Factor pricing refers to the prices of various factors (like land, labor, capital and entrepreneurship) of production, which is decided on the basis of market forces, i.e. demand, supply, and income which are micro variables.

3. Which of the following economic activities are included in the subject-matter of Economics?
    - **A.** Economic Activities related to Unlimited Wants
    - **B.** Economic Activities related to Limited Resources
    - **C.** Both A and B
    - **D.** None of these

Answer: C

Explanation:
"Economic Activities related to Unlimited Wants" and "Economic Activities related to Limited Resources" are included in the subject-matter of Economics.

4. 'Micros', which means 'Small' belongs to:
    - **A.** Arabian word
    - **B.** Greek word
    - **C.** German word
    - **D.** English word

Answer: B

Explanation:
'Micros', which means 'Small' belongs to Greek word.

5. Which of the following is true?
    - **A.** Human wants are infinite
    - **B.** Resources are limited
    - **C.** Scarcity problem gives birth to choice
    - **D.** All of these

Answer: C

Explanation:
Scarcity of resources gives rise to the fundamental economic problem of choice. As a society cannot produce enough goods and services to satisfy all the wants of its people, it has to make choices. ADVERTISEMENTS: A decision to produce one good requires a decision to produce less of some other good.

6. Which of the following is the salient feature of factors (or resources)?
- **A.** These are limited as compared to wants
- **B.** These have alternative uses
- **C.** Both A and B
- **D.** None of the above

Answer: C

Explanation:

"These are limited as compared to wants" and "These have alternative uses" is the salient feature of factors (or resources).

7. Which is a central problem of an economy?
- **A.** Allocation of Resources
- **B.** Optimum Utilisation of Resources
- **C.** Economic Development
- **D.** All of these

Answer: D

Explanation:

Allocation of Resources, Optimum Utilisation of Resources and Economic Development is a central problem of an economy.

8. Which of the following is a type of economic activities?
- **A.** Production
- **B.** Consumption
- **C.** Exchange and Investment
- **D.** All of these

Answer: D

Explanation:

Economic activity deals with the production, distribution, consumption and exchange of economic goods which are scarce in nature as compared to their demand and also those goods which have the utility to satisfy human wants.

9. To which factor, economic problem is basically related to?
- **A.** Choice
- **B.** Consumer's Selection
- **C.** Firm Selection
- **D.** None of these

Answer: A

Explanation:

An economic problem generally means the problem of making choices that occurs because of the scarcity of resources. It arises because people have unlimited desires but the means to satisfy that desire is limited.

10. Economy may be classified as:
- **A.** Capitalist
- **B.** Socialist
- **C.** Mixed
- **D.** All of these

Answer: D

Explanation:

A capitalist economy is characterized by private ownership of factors of production, while a socialist economy is characterized by state ownership of factors of production. A mixed economy, on the other hand, is characterized by private and state ownership of factors of production.

11. Which economy has a co-existence of private and public sectors?
- **A.** Capitalist
- **B.** Socialist
- **C.** Mixed
- **D.** None of these

Answer: C

Explanation:

A mixed economy is defined by the co-existence of a public and private sector.

12. The main aim of a socialist economy is________.
- **A.** Maximum production
- **B.** Economic freedom
- **C.** Earning profit
- **D.** To achieve social welfare

Answer: D

Explanation:

Socialists aim to achieve greater equality in decision-making and economic affairs, which means social welfare and equal rights of all must be achieved.

13. In which economy decisions are taken on the basis of price mechanism?
- **A.** Socialist
- **B.** Capitalist
- **C.** Mixed
- **D.** All of these

Answer: B

Explanation:

In a capitalist economic system, economic decision-making happens through price mechanisms as determined by markets. Price mechanism refers to the system where the forces of demand and supply determine the prices of commodities and the changes therein.

14. The slope of a production possibility curve falls:

A. from left to right	**B.** from right to left
C. from top to bottom	**D.** from bottom to top

Answer: C

Explanation:

The slope of a production possibility curve falls from top to bottom.

15. Production Possibility Curve is:

A. Concave to the axis	**B.** Convex to the axis
C. Parallel to the axis	**D.** Vertical to the axis

Answer: A

Explanation:

Production possibility curve (PPC) is concave to the origin because marginal opportunity cost (Loss of output of YGain of output of X) of shifting resources from commodity Y to commodity X tends to rise. This happens because resources are use-specific.

Chapter – 2   Consumer's Equilibrium and Demand

Meaning

The term equilibrium defines a state of rest from where there is no tendency to change anything. A consumer is observed to be in the state of equilibrium when he/she does not aspire to change his/her level of consumption i.e. when he/she attains maximum satisfaction. Therefore, consumer equilibrium refers to the situation when the consumer has attained maximum possible satisfaction from the number of commodities purchased given his/her income and price of the commodity in the market.

Consumer Equilibrium

A consumer is said to be in an equilibrium state when he feels that he cannot change his situation either by earning more or by spending more or by changing the number of things he buys. A rational consumer will purchase a commodity up to the point where the price of the commodity is equivalent to the marginal utility obtained from the thing. If this condition is not fulfilled, the consumer will either purchase more or less. If he purchases more, the MU will fall and situations will arise when the price paid will exceed marginal utility. In order to prevent negative utility, i.e. dissatisfaction, he will reduce his consumption and MU will go on increasing till price = marginal utility.

On the other hand, if marginal utility is greater than the price paid, the consumer will enjoy additional satisfaction from the unit he has consumed beforehand. This will urge him to buy more and more units of commodity leading to successive falls in MU till it gets equal to price. Hence, by buying more or less quantity, a consumer will eventually reach a point where P= MU. Here, his total utility is maximum.

Consumer
A consumer is an economic agent who consumes final goods or services for a consideration.

Utility
Utility is wanting satisfying power of a commodity.

Total utility
Total utility It is the total satisfaction derived from consumption of given quantity of a commodity at a given time. In other words, It is the sum of total of marginal utility.

Marginal Utility
Marginal Utility It is the change in total utility resulting from the consumption of an additional unit of the commodity.In other words, It is the utility derived from each additional unit.
$Mu_n = Tu_n - Tu_n - 1$

Relation between total utility and marginal utility

Units	Mu	Tu
1	10	10
2	8	18
3	6	24
4	4	28
5	2	30
6	0	30
7	-2	28

- When Mu diminishes but positive Tu increases at a diminishing rate.
- When Mu is zero, Tu is maximum.
- When Mu is negative, Tu diminishes.

Law of Diminishing Marginal Utility
As consumer consumes more and more units of commodity the Marginal utility derived from each successive units go on declining. This is the basis of law of demand.

Condition of Consumer's Equilibrium

According to this approach utility can be measured. "Utils" is the unit of utility.

Conditions:

- In case of one community

$$MUm = \frac{Mux}{Px} \; [\text{If } MUm = 1, MUx = Px]$$

Where, MUm = Marginal utility of money
MUx = Marginal utility of 'x', Px = Price of 'x'

- In case of two commodities.

$$\frac{MUx}{Px} = \frac{MUy}{Py} = MUm$$

xy and MU must be decreasing.

Units	MUx	MUy	MUx/Px	MUy/Py
1	36	40	12	10
2	33	36	11	**9**
3	30	32	10	8
4	27	28	**9**	7
5	24	24	8	6
6	21	20	7	5

Assumption, Px= Rs.3
Py=Rs.4
Y=Rs.20 Here, MUm= 9

Indifference curve analysis of consumer's equilibrium

An indifference curve depicts all the combinations of two goods that provide the consumer with equal satisfaction. When the Budget line is tangent to the indifference curve, a consumer will be in equilibrium, according to the indifference curve approach.

Characteristics of Indifference curves (IC)

- Indifference curves are negatively sloped (i.e. slopes downward from left to right).
- Indifference curves are convex to the point of origin. It is due to diminishing marginal rate of substitution.
- Indifference curves never touch or intersect each other. Two points on different IC cannot give equal level of satisfaction.
- Higher indifference curve represents higher level of satisfaction.

Consumer's Budget

It is a quantitative combination of two goods which can be purchased by a consumer from his given income.
Law of equi-marginal utility- It states that when a consumer spends his income on different commodity he will attain equilibrium or maximize his satisfaction at that point where ratio between marginal utility and price of different commodities are equal and which in turn is equal to marginal utility of money.

Budget set

It is quantitative combination of those bundles which a consumer can purchase from his given income at prevailing market prices.

Budget Line

A graphical representation of all those bundles which cost the amount just equal to the consumers money income gives us the budget line.

Preferences of the consumer

Consumer's preferences are called monotonic when between any two bundles, one bundle has more of one good and no less of other good as it offers him a higher level of satisfaction.

Indifference Curve

An indifference curve is a graphical representation of a combined products that gives similar kind of satisfaction to a consumer thereby making them indifferent.Every point on the indifference curve shows that an individual or a consumer is indifferent between the two products as it gives him the same kind of utility.

Indifference Curve Analysis

The indifference curve analysis work on a simple graph having two-dimensional. Each individual axis indicates a single type of economic goods. If the graph is on the curve or line, then it means that the consumer has no preference for any goods, because all the good has the same level of satisfaction or utility to the consumer. For instance, a child might be indifferent while having a toy, two comic book, four toy trucks and a single comic book.

Indifference Map

The Indifference Map refers to a set of Indifference Curves that reflects an understanding and gives an entire view of a consumer's choices. The below diagram shows an indifference map with three indifference curves.

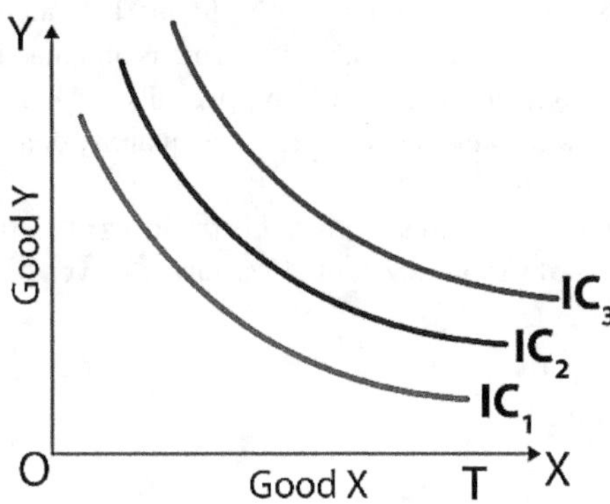

Theory of Demand

Demand is the number of goods or commodities, which a consumer is both, willing, and able to buy, at each possible price during a given period of time.

The definition of demand highlights four essential elements of demand:
- Quantity of the commodity
- Willingness of consumer to buy the commodity
- Price of the commodity at each given level of Quantity of the commodity
- Period of time

Market Demand

Market demand describes the demand for a given product and who wants to purchase it. This is determined by how willing consumers are to spend a certain price on a particular good or service. As market demand increases, so does price. When the demand decreases, price will go down as well.

Determinants of Market demand
- **Size and composition of Population**

Market demand for a commodity is affected by size of population in the country. Increase in population in the country. Increase in population in the country. Increase in population raises the market demand, while decrease in population reduces the market demand. Composition of population i.e. ratio of males, females, children and number of old people in the population also affects the demand for a commodity. For example :- if a market has larger proportion of women, then there will be more demand for articles of their use such as lipstick, sarees etc.

- **Season and weather**

The seasonal and weather conditions also affect the market demand for a commodity. For example : – during winters, demand for woolen clothes and jackets increases, whereas, market demand for raincoat and umbrellas increases during the rainy season.

- **Distribution of Income**

If income in the country is equitably distributed, then market demand for commodities will be more. However if income distribution is uneven i.e. people are either very rich or very poor, then market demand will remain at lower level.

Demand schedule

Demand schedule is a tabular statement showing various quantities of a commodity being demand at various levels of price, during a given period of time. It shows the relationship between price of the commodity and its quantity demanded.

A demand schedule can be determined both for individual buyers and for the entire market. So, demand schedule is of two types:

1. **Individual demand schedule**

    Individual demand schedule refers to a tabular statement showing various quantities of a commodity that a consumer is willing to buy at various levels of price, during a given period of time.

2. **Market demand schedule**

    Market demand schedule refers to a tabular statement showing various quantities of a commodity that all the consumers are willing to buy at various levels of price, during a given period of time.

Demand Curve

Let us assume that A and B are two consumers for commodity x in the market Table shows that market demand schedule is obtained by horizontally summing the individual demand. Market demand is obtained by adding demand of households A and B at different prices. At ₹ 5 per unit, market demand is 3 units. When price falls to ₹ 4, market demand rises to 5 units. So, market demand schedule also shows the inverse relationship between price and quantity demanded.

Demand curve is a graphical representation of demand schedule. It is the locus of all the points showing various quantities of a commodity that a consumer is willing to buy at various levels of price, during a given period of time, assuming no change in other factors.

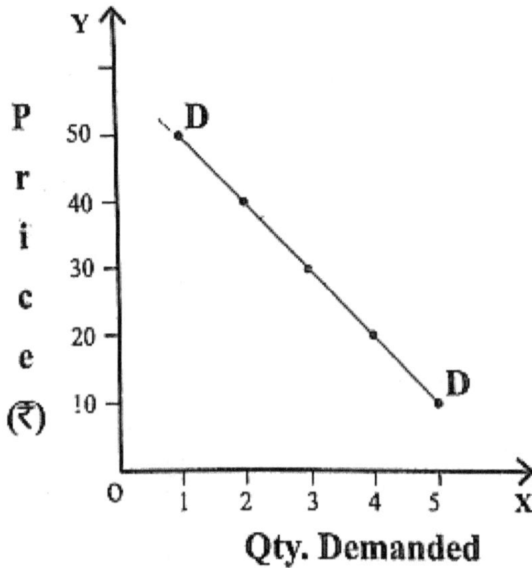

As we can see, the X-axis represents the quantity demanded of commodity X, and the Y-axis shows the price of commodity X. DD is the demand curve. The demand curve slope is left to the right downward sloping straight line. The demand curve slope is negative due to the inverse relationship between price and demand.

Movement along the Demand Curve

The change in both factors, namely the price and quantity demanded, from one point to the next is depicted by movement along the demand curve. There are two forms of movement in a demand curve: extension and contraction.

*   When the demand for a commodity rises due to a decrease in price, the demand curve extends. A contraction in the demand curve occurs when the demand for a commodity diminishes due to a price increase.

If the quantity changes due to the fluctuation in the price of the product or service, the demand curve moves. Any of the two directions of movement along the curve are possible:

*   Upward Movement indicates a decrease in demand, i.e., a decrease in demand due to a price increase.
*   Downward Movement indicates an increase in demand, i.e., demand for the product or service rises as prices decrease.

As a result, when prices are low, more of a good is demanded, whereas when prices are high, less quantity is demanded.

A Shift in the Demand Curve

A shift in the demand curve shows changes in demand at each potential price due to changes in one or more non-price factors like the price of comparable commodities, income, taste and preferences, and consumer expectations. If there is a shift in the demand curve, the equilibrium point also shifts. Any of the two sides of the demand curve shifts:

*   Rightward Shift denotes a rise in demand at the same price due to a favourable shift in non-price variables.
*   Leftward Shift: When the price remains constant, but other factors move unfavourably, this indicates a drop in demand.

Factors causing a Shift in the Demand Curve

The curve will shift to the right if consumers' desire to buy increases. It will shift to the left if consumer willingness to buy declines. The following are the most prominent causes of demand curve shifts:

- **Price of Related Goods:** An increase in demand for one product may impact demand for another. A rise in the price of pizzas, on the other hand, may stimulate demand for hamburgers.
- **Income:** As customers' incomes rise, so does their demand for things. On the other hand, as consumer earnings rise, demand for lower-quality goods will fall.
- **Numbers of Buyers:** Changes in the composition of the population have an impact on the demand for specific items.
- **Expectations:** Consumers' future expectations influence their purchasing decisions.

Demand Price Elasticity

The concept of price elasticity of demand (PED) is crucial in economic demand law. It is a measure of how price changes affect a product's demand. In other words, price elasticity of demand (PED) is a method for determining consumer responsiveness to price fluctuations, as opposed to price elasticity of supply, which determines supply responsiveness to price.

The price elasticity coefficient is almost always negative because the quantity demanded decreases with a price. Economists usually express the coefficient as a positive number even when it has the opposite meaning. However, it is important to note that a decrease in quantity demanded does not automatically imply a decrease in revenue. The increased profit margin could compensate for the slight decrease in purchases.

Price elasticity of demand formula (PED) = % change in quantity demanded / % change in price.

When a good's price elasticity is less than one, it would seem to be inelastic. In other words, a one-unit price increase results in a one-unit decrease in demand. The good is elastic if the correlation (absolute value) is larger than one. Therefore, a rise in price per unit will result in an even larger drop in demand. In theory, revenue is maximised when a good's price elasticity is one, and demand is unit elastic.

Different types of Price elasticity of demands

- **Perfectly Elastic Demand**

  Perfectly elastic demand occurs when a minor change in the price of a product produces a large change in its demand. In the case of completely elastic demand, a tiny increase in price leads to a drop in demand to zero, whereas a small decrease in price generates an increase in demand to infinity. The demand is completely elastic in this instance, or ep = 00.

- **Perfectly inelastic Demand**

  Completely inelastic demand occurs when there is no change in a product's demand in response to a price adjustment. The numerical value for perfectly inelastic demand (ep=0) is zero.

- **Relatively Elastic Demand**

  Relatively elastic demand occurs when the proportionate change in demand exceeds the corresponding change in the price of a product. Relatively elastic demand has a numerical value ranging from one to infinity.

- **Relatively Inelastic Demand**

  Relatively inelastic demand occurs when the percentage change in demand created is smaller than the percentage change in a product's price. For example, if the price of a product rises by 30% and demand falls by only 10%, the demand is said to be relatively inelastic. The numerical value of moderately elastic demand (ep1) varies from zero to one. Marshall defines moderately inelastic demand as elasticity less than one.

- **Unitary Elastic Demand**

  When a proportionate change in demand results in the same change in product price, the demand is said to be unitary elastic. Unitary elastic demand has a numerical value of one (ep=1).

Factors affecting Price Elasticity of Demand

Several common factors frequently influence whether a product has elastic or inelastic PED, such as:

- **Uniqueness:** Product lines with few or no alternative solutions are more likely to be inelastic. New products, for example, are much more likely to be inelastic and can be economical in several ways. Prices will need to be reduced as market conditions change and supply becomes more elastic.

- **Essentialness:** Products deemed necessary by consumers are more likely to be inelastic because they are prepared to pay more to acquire them. Bread and milk, for example, are deemed vital by many consumers, whereas soft drinks and cocoa are considered more 'optional' and have elastic demand.
- **Loyalty:** Products driven by customer loyalty are more likely to have inelastic demand because loyal customers are less price-sensitive.

Measurement of Price Elasticity of Demand

The price elasticity of demand is a calculation of the degree of change in a commodity's demand with respect to the price change of that commodity. The price elasticity of demand, in other words, is the rate of change in the quantity requested in response to the price change. It is sometimes denoted by Ep or PED. To understand the meaning of elasticity of demand, it is important to learn the methods of measuring the quantity.

Here, we will study the relative elasticity of demand types: price elasticity of demand, price elasticity formula, the elasticity of demand and supply, point elasticity of demand, etc.

Methods of Measuring Price Elasticity of Demand

Basically, there are four ways by which we can calculate the price elasticity of demand, and these are:
- Percentage method
- Total outlay method
- Point method
- Arc method

Percentage Method- Price Elasticity Demand

The Percentage method is one of the widely used methods for calculating demand price elasticities, where price elasticity is calculated in terms of the rate of the percentage change in the quantity requested to the percentage change in price.
The price elasticity of demand can, according to this approach, be mathematically expressed as:
PED = % change in quantity demanded / % change in price, where

$$\text{Change in quantity demanded} = \frac{\text{New quantity } (Q_2) - \text{Initial quantity } (Q_1)}{\text{Initial quantity } (Q_1) \times 100}$$

$$\text{Change in price} = \frac{\text{New price } (P2) - \text{Initial price } (P1)}{\text{Initial price } (P1) \times 100}$$

$$\text{Therefore, } PED = \frac{\Delta Q}{\Delta P} \times \frac{P1}{Q1}$$

Total outlay method

Total outlay is another method to measure elasticity of demand this is also known as the expenditure method, Total outlay is calculated by taking into account the total expenditure which Is price multiplied by quantity.

Point method

The point method evaluates jobs by comparing compensable factors - elements of job content like skill, effort or responsibility that can be used to assess a job's value to the organization. Each factor is defined and assigned a range of points based on the factor's relative importance to the organization.

Arc method

Arc elasticity is the sensitivity of one variable to another between two points on a curve. It is often used in the context of the law of demand to measure the inverse relationship between price and demand. Arc elasticity measures the responsiveness of demand to price changes over a range of values.

Change of Demand

- **Change in quantity Demanded or Movement along Demand curve**
  The following points are noteworthy so far as the difference between demand and quantity demanded is concerned:
  - Demand is defined as the willingness of buyer and his affordability to pay the price for the economic good or service. Quantity Demanded represents an exact quantity (how much) of a good or service is demanded by consumers at a particular price.
  - Demand refers to the graphing of all the quantities that can be purchased at different prices. On the contrary, quantity demanded, is the actual amount of goods desired at a certain price.
  - When a person talks about increase or decrease in demand, it means the change in demand. Conversely, if a person talks about expansion or contraction of demand, he refers to the change in quantity demanded.

- Changes in demand are due to the factors other than price, i.e. income, the price of complementary goods, the price of substitutes, etc. On the other hand, changes in quantity demanded is due to price.
- Change in demand will result in the shift in the demand curve. As opposed to quantity demanded, where the change may lead to the movement along the demand curve.

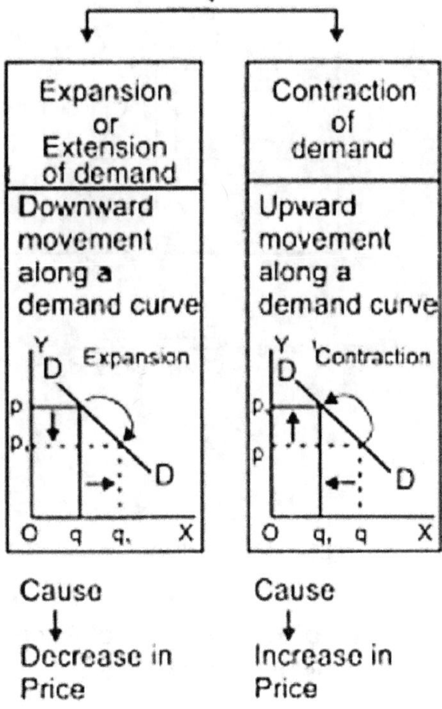

- **Change in Demand or Shift in Demand**

  Demand is defined as the quantity of a product or service, that a consumer is ready to buy at various prices, over a period. Demand Curve is a graph, indicating the quantity demanded by the consumer at different prices. The movement in demand curve occurs due to the change in the price of the commodity whereas the shift in demand curve is because of the change in one or more factors other than the price.

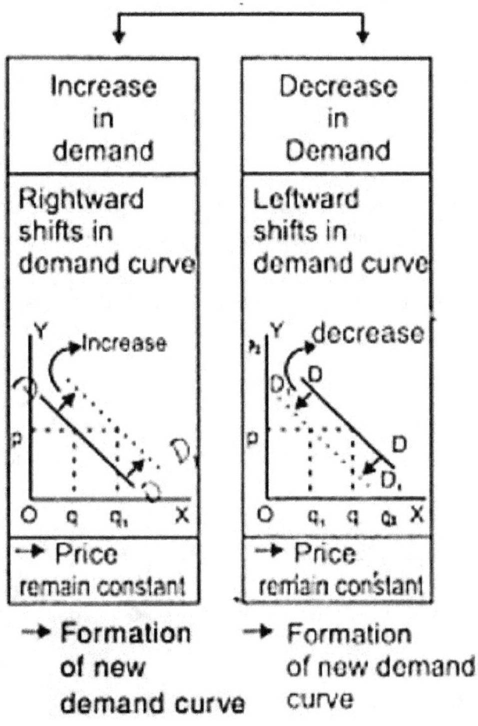

Demand curve and its slope

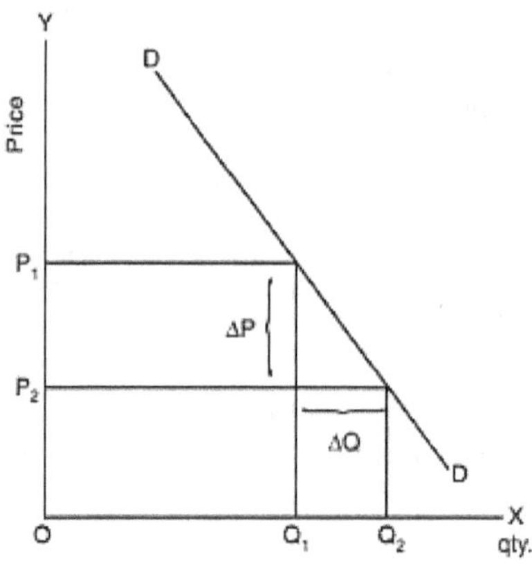

$$\text{slope of demand curve} = \frac{\text{Change in price}}{\text{Change in qty.dd.}}$$

$$= \frac{\Delta P}{\Delta Q}$$

Price Elasticity of Demand

Price Elasticity of Demand is a measurement of change in quantity demanded in response to a change in price of the commodity.

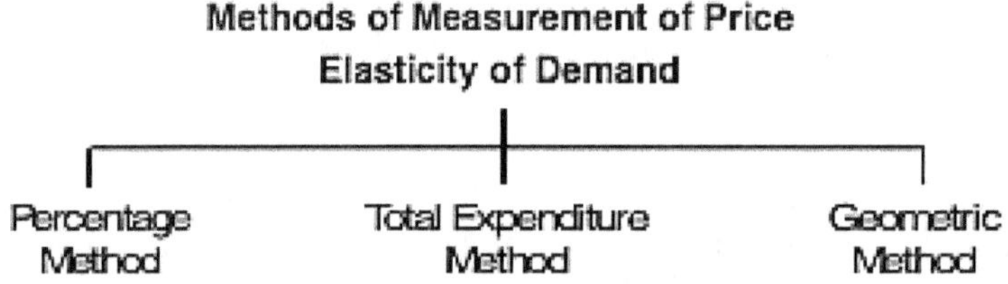

Multiple Choice Questions

1. Which of the following statements regarding utility is not true?
    - **A.** It helps consumers to make choices.
    - **B.** It is a satisfying power of a commodity.
    - **C.** Utility is always measurable.
    - **D.** It is purely a subjective entity.

Answer: C

Explanation:

Utility is a subjective concept and varies from person to person, at different times and at different places. There cannot be a standardized measure for utility. Therefore, the point that utility always measurable is not true.

2. __________ is the addition to total utility by the consumption of one additional unit of the commodity?
    - **A.** Marginal utility
    - **B.** Ordinal utility
    - **C.** Total utility
    - **D.** Average utility

Answer: A

Explanation:

Marginal utility is rate of change of total utility with respect to consumption of a commodity.so it is an addition to total utility resulting from a unit change in total utility.

3. Which of the following utility approaches suggests that utility is a measurable and quantifiable entity?
    - **A.** Cardinal approach
    - **B.** Ordinal approach
    - **C.** Both cardinal & ordinal
    - **D.** None of these

Answer: A

Explanation:

In cardinal utility approch utility is measured in numerical terms.And unit used for measurement is known as utils.

4. _________ shows various combinations of two goods that give same amount of satisfaction to the consumer.

A. Indifference curve	**B.** Isoquant
C. Isocost curve	**D.** Marginal utility curve

Answer: A

Explanation:

On indifference curve, consumer gets same satisfaction from each combination hence he is indifferent towards all combinations.

5. Indifference curve slopes_________?

A. Downward to the right	**B.** Downward to the left
C. Upward to the right	**D.** Upward to the left

Answer: A

Explanation:

In order to increase the consumption of one good,other good must be sacrificed as utility level through out the indifference cure has to be same.Due to inverse relation between two goods indifference curve slopes downwards to the right.

6. _________ is defined as the difference between what the consumer is willing to pay for a product and what he is able to pay?

A. Consumer surplus	**B.** Consumer burden
C. Price gap	**D.** Optimum price

Answer: A

Explanation:

Suppose a consumer is willing to pay Rs.10 for a commodity but it's price is Rs.6, we say that consumer's surplus is Rs.4. As per the concept of consumer surplus, a consumer is in equilibrium where consumer surplus is zero.Referring to above example when price of commodity is Rs.10 and consumer's surplus is zero, the consumer is said to be in equilibrium.

7. According to the law of diminishing marginal utility, _________?

A. After a point any addition in the consumption causes a reduction in total utility.	**B.** Additional consumption leads to lower average total utility
C. Additional consumption always yields extra utility	**D.** Additional consumption always yields negative utility

Answer: A

Explanation:

As per law of dimnishing marginal utility, as the consumer goes on conuming MU derived from each succesive unit goes on falling,becomes zero and finally turns negative

8. The want satisfying power of a commodity is known as:

A. Demand	**B.** Consumption
C. Supply	**D.** Utility

Answer: D

Explanation:

utility represents satisfaction experienced by the consumer from a good.

9. What is called point of satiety?

A. The point where marginal utility becomes greater than zero	**B.** The point where marginal utility becomes zero
C. The point where marginal utility becomes less than zero	**D.** None of above

Answer: B

Explanation:

Point of Satiety is defined as " the point where marginal utility of any commodity is zero". Thus it is a point where satisfaction of any commodity is zero.

10. The value of elasticity in case of a rectangular hyperbola demand curve will be:

A. One	**B.** Greater than one
C. Infinity	**D.** Less than one or greater than one

Answer: A

Explanation:

The rectangular hyperbola curve said to be unitary elastic as elasticity along the demand curve is same.

11. A consumer reaches equilibrium at the point where:

    A. MU is less than P   **B.** MU is greater than P

    C. MU=P   **D.** TU=P

Answer: C

Explanation:

To determine the equilibrium point, consumer compares the price (or cost) of the given commodity with its utility (satisfaction or benefit). Being a rational consumer, he will be at equilibrium when marginal utility is equal to price paid for the commodity.

12. Due to a 10 percent fall in the price of a good, its demand rises from 400 units to 450 units. Calculate its price elasticity of demand.

    A. 3.25.   **B.** 2.25

    C. 1.25   **D.** 4.25

Answer: C

Explanation:

using percentage method of calculating elasticity % change in quantity demanded = (50/400)*100 = 12.5% % change in price = 10% 12,5/10 = 1.25 =ed

13. The elasticity of demand on different points on a linear demand curve is different. It is:

    A. True   **B.** False

    C. Indefinite   **D.** Can't say

Answer: A

Explanation:

As per geomeric method for calculating price elasticity,we can say it can be different. slope remains constant as it is linear curve but not the elsaticity, it can be different.

14. What does monotonicity of preferences imply?

    A. Consumer always prefer bundle giving same satisfaction   **B.** Consumer will not prefer bundle giving maximum satisfaction

    C. Consumer always prefer bundle giving maximum satisfaction   **D.** Consumer always prefer bundle giving minimum satisfaction

Answer: C

Explanation:

An agent's preferences are said to be stronglymonotonic if, given a consumption bundle , the agent prefers all consumption bundles that have more of at least one good, and not less in any other good.

15. What will you say about MU when TU is maximum?

    A. It will be one   **B.** It will be zero

    C. It will be infinity   **D.** It will be negative

Answer: B

Explanation:

MU & TU relationship:

- MU is the rate of change of TU.
- When the MU decreases, TU increases at decreasing rate.
- When MU becomes zero, TU is maximum. It is a saturation point.
- When MU becomes negative, TU declines

16. Suppose a consumer's preferences are monotonic. What can you say about his preference ranking over the bundles (10,10), (10,9) and (9,9)?

    A. He will prefer (10,9)   **B.** He will prefer (10,10)

    C. He will prefer all   **D.** He will prefer (9,9)

Answer: D

Explanation:

A consumer's preferences are said to be stronglymonotonic if, given a consumption bundle , the consumer prefers all consumption bundles that have more of at least one good, and not less in any other good.

17. Suppose the price elasticity of demand for a good is – 0.2. How will the expenditure on the good be affected if there is a 10 % increase in the price of the good?

    A. Expenditure will not change   **B.** Expenditure will increase

    C. Expenditure will decrease   **D.** Expenditure will remain same

Answer: B
Explanation:
As per total outlay method:
- If with a fall in price (demand increases) the total expenditure increases or with a rise in price (demand falls), the total expenditure falls, in that case the elasticity of demand is greater than one i.e. ED > 1.
- If with a rise or fall in the price (demand falls or rises respectively), the total expenditure remains the same, the demand will be unitary elastic or ED = 1.
- If with a fall in price (Demand rises), the total expenditure also falls, and with a rise in price (Demand falls) the total expenditure also rises, the demand is said to be less classic or elasticity of demand is less than one (ED < 1).

18. Price elasticity of demand for wheat is equal to unity and a household demands 40 Kg of wheat when the price is Rs.1 per kg. At what price will the household demand 20 kg of wheat?

A. 6	**B.** 4
C. 1.5	**D.** 5

Answer: C
Explanation:
If elasticity of demand is equal to 1. then, % change in price = % change in quantity there is 50% fall in quantity from 40 to 20 kg. hence there should be 50% increase in price new price = 1.5

19. Which of the following law states that the more a consumer consumes of a product the less is the utility he derives from the additional consumption?

A. Law of cardinal utilit	**B.** Law of diminishing marginal utility
C. Law of ordinal utility	**D.** Law of equi-marginal utility

Answer: B
Explanation:
Law of diminishing marginal utility states that the more a consumer consumes of a product the less is the utility he derives from the additional consumption.

20. _________ is the rate at which a consumer is willing to substitute one good for the other maintaining the same level of utility?

A. Income effect	**B.** Substitution effect
C. Marginal rate of substitution	**D.** Increasing marginal utility

Answer: C
Explanation:
The marginal rate of substitution (MRS) is the rate at which a consumer can give up some amount of one good in exchange for another good while maintaining the same level of utility. At equilibrium consumption levels (assuming no externalities), marginal rates of substitution are identical.

21. How would you calculate the new partner's capital, when it is not given in the question?

A. Old partners capital after adjustment x reciprocal of old partner's share × sacrificing share	**B.** Old partners capital after adjustment x reciprocal of sacrificing share × new partner's share
C. Price of the two goods	**D.** Old partners capital after adjustment x reciprocal of remaining share x new partner's share

Answer: D
Explanation:
Calculation of new partner's capital should be done as follows:
- Calculated the combined or adjusted capitals of all the existing partners (after all adjustments)
- Find out the reciprocal of remaining share
- Now, combined capitals x reciprocal of remaining share x new partner's share

22. The total utility divided by the number of units consumed is known as?

A. Total utility	**B.** Marginal utility
C. Average utility	**D.** None of above

Answer: C
Explanation:
Average utility is nothing but utility derived by per unit of consumption.

23. According to Marshall, the law of diminishing marginal utility applies on _________?

    A. Bank money

    B. Money in the same manner as it applies on the commodity

    C. Cash but not on bank money

    D. All commodities except money

Answer: D

Explanation:

According to Marshall, The law of diminishing marginal utility states that as a person consumes more and more units of a commodity, the utility or satisfaction derived from each additional unit decreases. This law applies to all commodities except money.

24. The coefficient of price elasticity of demand is always:

    A. Zero

    B. Positive

    C. Negative

    D. Undefined

Answer: C

With a downward-sloping demand curve, price and quantity demanded move in opposite directions, so the price elasticity of demand is always negative. A positive percentage change in price implies a negative percentage change in quantity demanded, and vice versa.

25. When total utility increases, marginal utility is _________.

    A. Negative and declining

    B. Negative and increasing

    C. Zero

    D. Positive and declining

Answer: D

Explanation:

Relationship between Total Utility and Marginal Utility :

1. TU increases with an increase in consumption of a commodity as long as MU is positive. In this phase, TU increases but a diminishing rate as MU from each successive unit tends to diminish.

2. When TU reaches its maximum, MU becomes zero. TU stops rising at this stage. This point is known as point of satiety.

3. When consumption is increased beyond the point of satiety, TU starts falling as MU becomes negative.

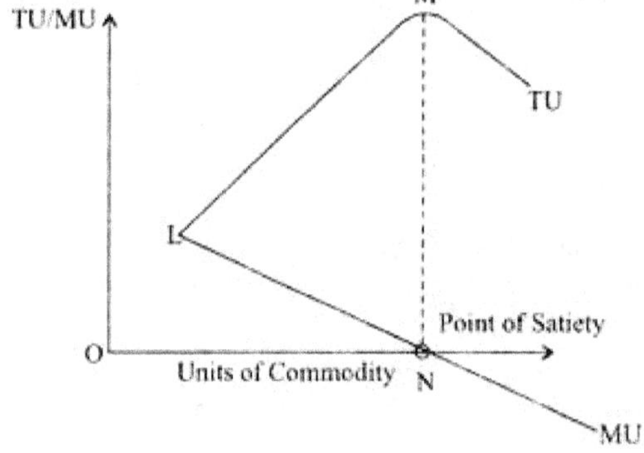

26. At the point of tangency, the slope of the indifference curve is _________.

    A. Greater than the price line

    B. Less than the price line

    C. The same as the price line

    D. None of these

Answer: C

Explanation:

At the point of tangency, the slope of the indifference curve is the same as the price line.

27. A movement along a given indifference curve is known as:

    A. Price effect

    B. Substitution effect

    C. Income effect

    D. None of above

Answer: B

Explanation:

The substitution effect measures the change in consumption such that the consumer's level of utility does not change. The substitution effect can, therefore, be thought of as a movement along the same indifference curve.

28. Consumer surplus is more in the case of _______.

    A. Comforts

    B. Necessities

    C. Inferior goods

    D. Luxuries

Answer: A

Explanation:

Consumer surplus is a measure of the welfare that people gain from consuming goods and servicesConsumer surplus is defined as the difference between the total amount that consumers are willing and able to pay for a good or service (indicated by the demand curve) and the total amount that they actually do pay . As per Alferd marshall ,CS can not be calculated for luxary goods, inferior goods and necessities.

29. Which of the following curve has a negative slope and cannot interest each other?

    A. Isoquants   **B.** Indifference curves

    C. Demand and supply curves   **D.** None of above

Answer: B

Explanation:

IC slopes downward because as the consumer increases the consumption of one commodity, he has to give up certain units of other commodity in order to maintain the same level of satisfaction. two indifference curves represent two different levels of satisfaction. If these indifference curves intersect each other, the intersection will represent same level of satisfaction, which is impossible.

30. When the income elasticity of demand is greater than unity, the commodity is ______.

A. anecessity   **B.** a luxury

C. an inferior good   **D.** a non-related good

Answer: B

Explanation:

A negative income elasticity of demand is associated with inferior good.

A positive income elasticity of demand is associated with normal good.

For a necessary good, income elasticity of demand of a commodity is less than 1 but greater than 0.

For a luxury or superior good, elasticity of demand is greater than 1.

Chapter – 3   Producer Behaviour & Supply

Meaning

Production function means a mathematical equation/representation of the relationship between tangible inputs and the tangible output of a firm during the production of goods. A single factor in the absence of the other three cannot help production. In simple words, it describes the method that will enable the maximum production of goods by technically combining the four major factors of production- land, enterprise, labor and capital at a certain timeframe using a specific technology most efficiently. It changes with development in technology. J H Von was the first person to develop the proportions of the first variable of this function in the 1840s

Production function

The production function of a firm is a relationship between inputs used and output produced by the firm. For various quantities of inputs used, it gives the maximum quantity of output that can be produced. It shows the functional relation between physical inputs and physical output of a good. It can be expressed as $Q = (f_1, f_2, f_3 \dots f_n)$. Where Q = Physical output of a good; $f_1, f_2, f_3, \dots \dots f_n$ = Physical inputs. Technology remains constant.

The inputs that a firm uses in the production process are called factors of production. In order to produce output, a firm may require any number of different inputs. However, for the time being, here we consider a firm that produces output using only two factors of production – labour and capital. Our production function, therefore, tells us the maximum quantity of output (q) that can be produced by using different combinations of these two factors of productionsLabour (L) and Capital (K). We may write the production function as q = f(L,K) where, L is labour and K is capital and q is the maximum output that can be produced.

Production Function

Factor		Capital						
		0	1	2	3	4	5	6
Labour	0	0	0	0	0	0	0	0
	1	0	1	3	7	10	12	13
	2	0	3	10	18	24	29	33
	3	0	7	18	30	40	46	50
	4	0	10	24	40	50	56	57
	5	0	12	29	46	56	58	59
	6	0	13	33	50	57	59	60

Types of Production Function

There are two types of Production Function.
1. **Short-run Production Function:** In this production function one factor of production is variable and all others are fixed. So, law of return to a factor is applied. It is also called variable proportion type production function. he short run production function considers the change in the level of output when only one variable is changeable and other variables are kept constant.
2. **Long-run Production Function:** In this production function all the factors of production are variable. So, law of returns to scale is applied. It is also called constant proportion type production function. In the case of the long-run production function, the variables are changed proportionally.

Difference between short run & long run

Basis	Short Run	Long Run
Meaning	Only variable factors are changed	All factors are changed
Price Determination	Demand is active.	Both demand & supply play an important role.
Classification	Factors are classified as fixed & variable.	All factors are variable.

- **Total production:** Total production refers to the total amount of a good which is produced by a firm in a given period of time.
- **Average production:** Average production is the per unit output of variable factor (Labour) employed.

$$AP = \frac{TP}{\text{Units of Variable input}}$$

- **Marginal product:** Marginal product is the change in total product resulting from employing one additional unit of variable input.

$$MP = \frac{\Delta TP}{\Delta L} \text{ or } MP_n = TP_n - TP_{n-1}$$

Relation between Total, Average and Marginal Product

1. As long as marginal product rises, total product increases at increasing rate.
2. When marginal product starts falling but remains positive, total product rises at diminishing rate.
3. When MP = 0, TP is maximum.
4. When marginal product becomes negative, then total product starts falling.

Relation betwen MP and AP

- When MP > AP, AP rises.
- When MP = AP, AP is maximum and constant.
- When MP < AP, AP falls.

Returns to a factor

In a short period when additional unit of variable factor are employed with fixed factors, then returns to a factor operates. Returns to a factor shows the changes in total product of a good when only the quantity of one input is increased, while other inputs kept constant.

Law of variable proportion

The law states that as we increase the quantity of only one variable input, keeping other inputs fixed, the total product increases at increasing rate in the beginning, then increases at decreasing rate and finally TP falls. According to this law, change in TP and MP are classify into three phases.

Phase I: TP Increases at increasing rate: In the initial phase as more and more units of variable factor are employed with fixed factor total physical production increases at increasing rate, MP increases.

Phase II: TP increases at decreasing rate: As more and more units of variable factors are employed with fixed factors then total product increases at diminishing rate, MP decreases but remains positive. At the end of this phase TP maximum and MP becomes zero.

Phase III: TP falls: As more and more units of variable factors are employed with fixed factors, total production starts decreasing and marginal product becomes negative.

Cost

It is the sum of direct (explicit cost) and indirect cost (explicit cost), including Normal profit.

Cost = Explicit cost + implicit cost + Normal Profit.

Short run costs

The short-run cost comprises both the fixed cost (that do not differ with the change in the degree of end results) and variable cost (that differs with the changes in the level of degree of end results). Some factors remain constant or fixed due to the time restrictions forced on an establishment.

Total cost

Total cost refers to total expenditure incurred by a firm on production of a given quentity of output.

- Total cost is the sum of total fixed cost and total variable cost TC = TFC + TVC or TC = AC × Q
- Total fixed costs is the cost which remains constant at all levels of output. It is not zero even at zero output level. Therefore, TFC curve is parallel to OX-axis.

  TFC = TC − TVC or TFC = AFC × Q
- Total variable cost is the cost which vary with the quantity of output produced. It is zero at zero level of output. TVC curve is parallel to TC curve.

  TVC = TC − TFC or TVC = AVC × Q.

Average Cost

The average cost is per unit cost of production of a commodity. It is the sum of average fixed cost and average variable cost.

$$AC = \frac{TC}{Q} \text{ or } AC = AFC + AVC$$

- The average fixed cost is per unit fixed cost of production of a commodity.

  $$AFC = \frac{TFC}{Q} \text{ or } AFC = AC - AVC$$

- AFC goes on decreasing as the level of output increase. Shape of AFC is rectangular hyperbola.
- Average variable cost is per unit variable cost of production of a commodity.

  $$AVC = \frac{TVC}{Q} \text{ or } AVC = AC - AFC$$

Marginal Cost

It refers to change in TC, due to an additional unit of a commodity is produced. $MC = \Delta TC/\Delta Q$ or $MC_n = TC_n - TC_{n-1}$ But under short run. it is calculated from TVC.

$$MC_n = TVC_n - TC_{n-1} \text{ or } MC = \frac{\Delta TVC}{\Delta Q}$$

Explicit Cost

Actual money expenditure incurred by a firm on the purchase and hiring the factor inputs for the production is called explicit cost. For example-payment of wages, rent, interest, purchases of raw materials etc.

Implicit cost

Implicit cost is the estimated cost of self-owned resources of the production used in production process, by the producer or estimated value of inputs supplied by owner itself.

Relation Between Short-Term Costs

- Total cost curve and total variable cost curve remains parallel to each other. The vertical distance between these two curves is equal to total fixed cost.

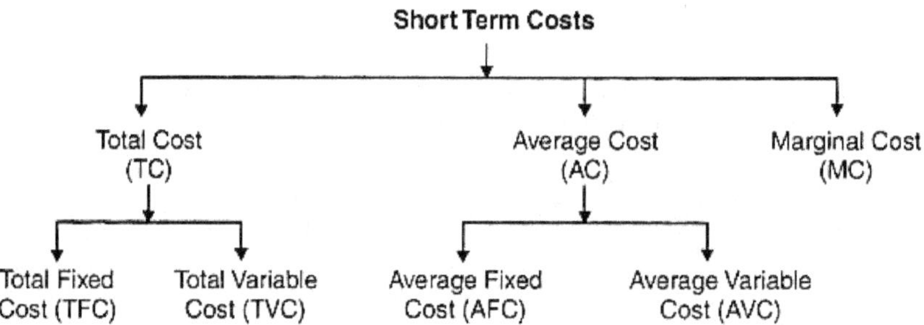

- TFC curve remains parallel to X-axis and TVC curve remains parallel to TC curve.
- With increase in level of output, the vertical distance between AFC curve and AC curve goes on increasing. On contrary the vertical distance between AC curve and AVC curve goes on decreasing because their difference is AFC which keep decreasing whith increase in output but these two curves never intersect because average fixed cost is never zero.
- **Relation between MC and AVC.**
- When MC < AVC, AVC falls.
- When MC = AVC, AVC is minimum and constant
- When MC > AVC, AVC rises.
- **Relation between MC and ATC**
- When MC < ATC, ATC falls.
- When MC = ATC, ATC is minimum and Constant
- When MC > ATC, ATC rises.

Revenue

Money received from the sale of a product is called revenue.

- Total revenue is the total amount of money received by a firm from the sale of given units of a commodity at a market price.

  $$TR = AR \times Q \text{ or } TR = \Sigma MR$$

  TR = Price × Quantity Sold.

  Price = AR

- Per unit revenue received from the sale of given units of a commodity is called average revenue. Average revenue is equal to price. Per unit price of a commodity is also called AR.

$$AR = \frac{TR}{Q} \text{ or } \frac{P \times Q}{Q} = P = Price$$

- Marginal revenue is net addition to total revenue when one additional unit of output is sold.

$$MR = \frac{\Delta TR}{\Delta Q} \text{ or } MR_n = TR_n - TR_{n-1}$$

- Relation between TR, AR and MR when more quantity sold at the same price : under perfect competition.
  - Average revenue and marginal revenue remains constant at all levels of output and AR and MR curves are parallel to ox-axis. AR = MR.
  - Total revenue increases at constant rate MR is constant and TR curve is positively sloped straight line passing through the origin.
- Relation between TR, AR and MR when more quantity by sold at the lower price or there is monopoly or monopolistic competition in the market.
  - Average revenue and marginal revenue curves have negative slope. MR curve lies below AR curve. AR > MR.
  - Marginal revenue falls, twice the rate of average revenue.
  - So long as marginal revenue decreases and positive, total revenue increases at diminishing rate. When marginal revenue is zero, total revenue is maximum and when marginal revenue becomes negative, TR starts falling.
- **Relation b/w AR and MR (General)**
  - When MR > AR, AR rises.
  - When MR = AR, AR is maximum and constant.
  - When MR < AR, AR falls.

Concept of Producer's Equilibrium

It refers the stage where producer is getting maximum profit or suffering minimum losses with given cost and he has no incentive to increase or decrease the level of output. A producer's equilibrium is the situation in which the Producer's profit is maximised due to the combination of price and output.

- **MR and MC Approach:** Conditions of producer equilibrium according to this approach are:
  - MC = MR
  - MC curve should cut the MR curve from below at the point of equilibrium.
                    Or
  MC should be more than MR after the equilibrium point, with increase in output.

- **Supply:** Refers to the amount of the commodity that a firm or seller is willing to offer or ready to sell at a certain price, over a given period of time.
- **Factors affecting supply of a commodity:**
  - Price of the commodity.
  - Prices of other related goods.
  - Level of Technology.
  - Prices of inputs.
  - No. of firms.
  - Government policy regarding Taxation and subsidies.
  - Goals of the firm.
- **Individual Supply:** Refers to quantity of a commodity that an individual firm is willing and able to offer for sale at a certain price during a given period of time.
- **Market supply:** It is the sum total of quantity supplied of a commodity by all sellers or all firms in the market at a certain price during a given period of time.
- **Stock:** Refers to the total quantity of a particular commodity available with the firm at a particular point of time.
- **Supply Schedule:** Refers to a tabular presentation which shows various quantities of a commodity that a producer is willing to supply at different prices, during a given period of time.
- **Supply curve:** Refers to the graphical representation of supply schedule which represents various quantities of a commodity that a producer is willing to supply at different prices during given period of time.
- Slope of supply curve = $\Delta P / \Delta Q$

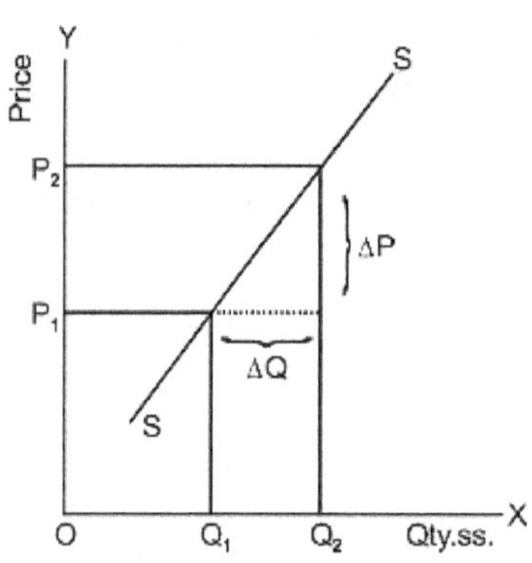

- **Law of Supply:** States the direct relationship between price and quantity of supply of a commodity, keeping other factors constant.
- **Price Elasticity of Supply:** It refers to the degree of responsiveness of quantity supplied of a commodity with reference to a change in price of the commodity. It is always positive due to direct relationship between price and quantity supplied.

$$\text{Price Elasticity of Supply (Es)} = \frac{\text{Percentage change in quantity supplied}}{\text{Percentage change in price}}$$

- **Methods for measuring price elasticity of supply:**
  Percentage Method

$$Es = \frac{\%\ \text{change in a quantity supplied}}{\%\ \text{change in price}}$$

$$\text{Or } Es = \frac{\Delta Q}{\Delta P} \times \frac{P}{Q}$$

Change in Quantity Supplied Vs change in Supply

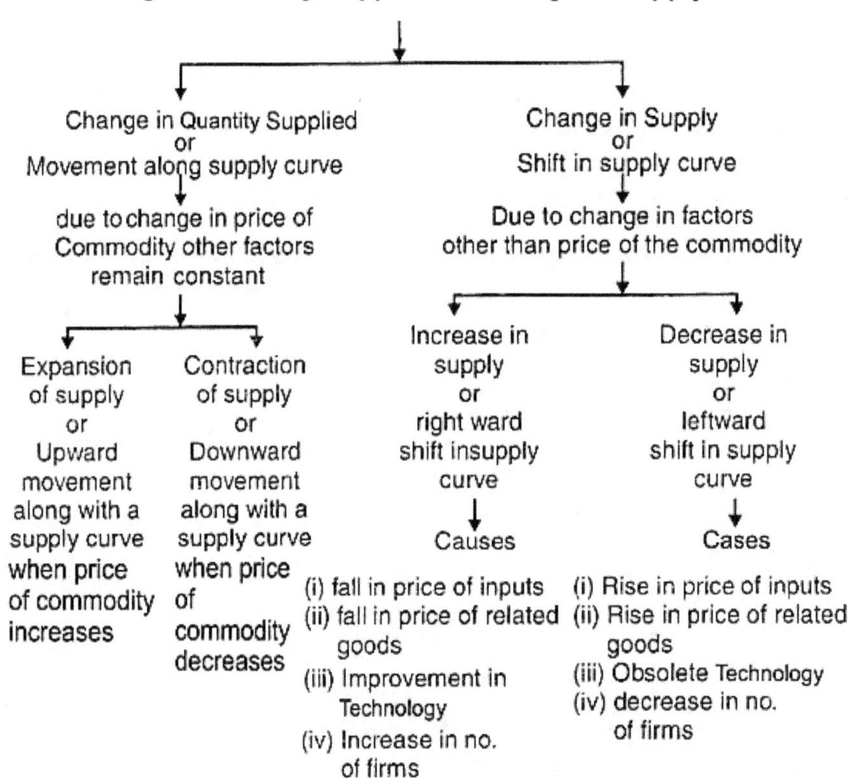

1. In the short run TPP changes with the change in which of the following factors:

    A. Variable factors   **B.** Fixed factors

    C. Economic cost   **D.** All the factors

Answer: A

Explanation:

In the short run, only the variable factors can be changed. Fixed factors cannot be changed in the short run.

2. In the long run TPP changes with the change in which of the following factors:

    A. Economic cost   **B.** Fixed factors

    C. Variable factors   **D.** All the factors

Answer: D

Explanation:

In the long run all the factors can be changed. All the factors (variable and fixed) become variable factors in the long run.

3. In short run which of the following factors can be changed easily:

    A. Variable factors   **B.** Fixed factors

    C. All the factors   **D.** None

Answer: A

In the short run variable factors like labour, raw materials can be changed easily. It is difficult to change fixed factors like land, machinery, equipments, etc in the short period as procuring/selling land or machinery or capital will take time and it is difficult to change them in the short period.

4. In short run TPP changes with the change in:

    A. Average product   **B.** Average cost

    C. Marginal Product   **D.** Total Product

Answer: C

Explanation:

The change in total product is due to the change brought about by an additional unit produced, which is the marginal product. Since fixed cost do not change, it is only the change in variable factors which is reflected in the marginal product. and the change in total product depends upon the change in marginal product.

5. The general shape of TPP in the short run is:

    A. Hyperbola   **B.** U shaped

    C. Inverse U shaped   **D.** V- shaped

Answer: C

Explanation:

It is inverse U shaped because the initially the total product increases at a increasing rate, and then it increases at a diminishing rate and finally the total product starts decreasing.

6. Money costs mean:

    A. Money spent by the consumers   **B.** Money expenditure on output

    C. Money expenditure of a producer in the production process   **D.** Money expenditure on purchase of goods from the factory

Answer: C

Explanation:

When production cost is expressed in terms of monetary units, it is called money cost.

7. Implicit costs are:

    A. Opportunity costs   **B.** Total cost

    C. Impute   **D.** Same as explicit costs

Answer: C

Explanation:

Implicit costs are impute. An implicit cost is any cost that has already occurred but not necessarily shown or reported as a separate expense. It represents an opportunity cost that arises when a company uses internal resources toward a project without any explicit compensation for the utilization of resources.

8. Opportunity cost is the:

    A. Next best alternative available   **B.** Next best alternative chosen

    C. Next best alternative sacrificed   **D.** Next best alternative produced

Answer: C

Explanation:

Opportunity cost is the next best alternative sacrificed. Opportunity cost is defined as the cost of the next best alternative foregone. It represents the sacrifices that people must make due to the scarcity of resources. Resources are limited but wants are unlimited, thus choices must be made.

9. Revenue for a firm is:

    A. Money receipts from the sale of output   **B.** Average price of a product sold

    C. Addition to Total revenue after a good is sold   **D.** Money spent on producing output

Answer: A

Explanation:

Total revenue refers to money receipts of a firm from the sale of its total output. It is estimated as the multiple of price and quantity of output.

10. The law of supply explains a:

    A. Positive relationship between Price of a commodity and quantity supplied   **B.** Positive relationship between Price of a commodity and supply

    C. Negative relationship between Price of a commodity and quantity supplied   **D.** Positive relationship between Price of a commodity and market supply

Answer: A

Explanation:

According to the law of supply there is a direct relationship between the price of the commodity and the qty supplied. If the price increases qty supplied increases and vice versa.

11. Market supply is best defined as:

    A. Horizontal summation of all individual quantity supplied at various prices   **B.** Vertical summation of all individual quantity supplied at various prices

    C. Vertical summation of all individual quantity supplied at a given price   **D.** Horizontal summation of all individual quantity supplied at a given price

Answer: A

Explanation:

Market supply is best defined as horizontal summation of all individual quantity supplied at various prices.

12. The supply curve of a firm shows:

    A. Graphical representation of quantity supplied at various profit levels   **B.** Graphical representation of quantity supplied at a particular price only

    C. Graphical representation of quantity supplied at various prices   **D.** Graphical representation of quantity supplied at keeping prices constant

Answer: C

Explanation:

It is the locus of all the points showing various quantities of a commodity that a producer is willing to sell at various levels of price.

13. The elasticity of supply measures:

    A. The degree of responsiveness of supply of a commodity with reference to change in price of such commodity.   **B.** The quantity supplied at a price

    C. The initial quantity supplied at the initial price   **D.** The difference in quantity supplied when price fall

Answer: A

Explanation:

It points to the reaction of the sellers to a particular change in the price of the commodity.

14. A supply schedule is best defined as:
   A. Tabular representation of quantity supplie
   B. Tabular representation of quantity supplied at keeping prices constant
   C. Graphical representation of quantity supplied at a particular price only
   D. Tabular representation of quantity supplied at various profit levels

Answer: A

Explanation:

Price	Quantity supplied
1	10
2	15
5	25

In this schedule we can see that as the price of the commodity increases , its supply also increases.

15. Explicit costs are paid to:
   A. Internal owners of factors
   B. External owners of factors
   C. The tax authorities
   D. The government

Answer: B

Explanation:

Explicit costs are normal business expenses that are easy to track and appear in the general ledger. Explicit costs are the only costs necessary to calculate a profit, as they clearly affect a company's profits. Wages that a firm pays its employees or rent that a firm pays for its office are explicit costs.

16. Marginal Revenue is:
   A. Addition to the total revenue on the sale of an additional unit of Output
   B. Addition to the total revenue on the production of an additional unit of Output
   C. Addition to the total revenue on the sale of an additional unit of Output
   D. Additional cost involved in production

Answer: C

Explanation:

Marginal Revenue is Addition to the total revenue on the sale of an additional unit of Output.

$MR_n = TR_n - TR_{n-1}$

17. Variable costs vary with output because:
   A. It changes on its own
   B. It does not remain constant in the long run
   C. It is impossible to keep them fixed
   D. It varies as it is the expenditure on the variable factors which can be changed in the short run

Answer: D

Explanation:

Variable costs vary with output because it varies as it is the expenditure on the variable factors which can be changed in the short run.

18. Average cost is derived by:
   A. Subtracting Total Cost by units of output
   B. Dividing Total Cost by units of output
   C. Multiplying Total Cost by units of output
   D. Adding Total Cost by units of output

Answer: B

Explanation:

It refers to the per unit cost of production. $AC = TC \div Q$

19. Explain the relationship TC, TFC & TVC.
   A. TVC+TFC= TC
   B. TVC-TFC= TC
   C. TVC × TFC= TC
   D. TVC/TFC=TC

Answer: A

Explanation:

TC is the sum of total fixed cost and total variable cost at various levels of output. Since TFC remains same at all levels of output the change in TC is entirely due to TVC. Therefore the vertical distance between TC and TFC curve is equal to TVC.

20. Diagrammatically AC has a U shape. The statement is:
   A. May be
   B. May not be
   C. True
   D. FALSE

Answer: C

Explanation:

The AC curve is U shaped as it initially falls with increase in output. Once the output rises till optimum level, AC starts rising.

21. The relationship between AC & MC is:

    A. AC continues to fall till MC is less than AC

    B. AC continues to fall till MC is equal to AC

    C. AC continues to rise till MC is less than AC

    D. AC continues to fall till MC is greater than AC

Answer: A

Explanation:

When MC <AC , AC falls When MC=AC , AC is constant and at ita minimum point When MC> AC, AC rises.

22. AFC curve never touches 'X' axis though it lies very close to X axis because:

    A. AFC is horizontal

    B. AFC can never be zero as TFC can never be zero

    C. AFC curve can never be extended to touch zero with increase in output

    D. AFC is always vertical

Answer: B

Explanation:

There is always an element of TFC even at zero kevel of output. Because of this reason AFC can never be zero and though it kies close to the X axus it can never touch the X axis.

23. AVC and AFC always lie below AC because:

    A. They are concave

    B. They are convex

    C. Their sum is equal to AC

    D. They are always downward sloping

Answer: C

Explanation:

AC curve will always lie above the AVC and AFC curve because AC , at all levels of output includes both AVC and AFC.

24. TVC curve starts from origin as:

    A. TVC is horizontal

    B. TVC is zero at zero level of output

    C. TVC is vertical curve from origin

    D. TVC slopes upward from the origin at higher level of output

Answer: B

Explanation:

TVC directly varies with the level of output. When there is no output, TVC will be zero, as at zero level of output, no raw materials will be needed, no labour charges have to be paid etc. So there will be no variable cost at zero level of output.

25. Which of the following explains the short-run production function?

    A. Law of Demand

    B. Law of Variable Proportion

    C. Returns to Scale

    D. Elasticity of Demand

Answer: B

Explanation:

Law of Variable Proportion is regarded as an important theory in Economics. It is referred to as the law which states that when the quantity of one factor of production is increased, while keeping all other factors constant, it will result in the decline of the marginal product of that factor.

26. Which of the following is the true meaning of opportunity cost?

    A. It is the next best alternative that is available in a given situation

    B. It is the next best alternative that is sacrificed in a given situation

    C. Both a and b are correct

    D. Both a and b are incorrect

Answer: B

Explanation:

"It is the next best alternative that is available in a given situation" and "It is the next best alternative that is sacrificed in a given situation" is the true meaning of opportunity cost

27. Which of the following economists gave the statement 'Supply creates its own demand'?

    A. Jean-Baptiste Say

    B. James Madison

    C. Thomas Jefferson

    D. None of the above

Answer: A

Explanation:

'Supply creates its own demand' was said by Jean-Baptiste Say. According to him whatever is produced is sold in the economy. The economy works on full employment level and its a normal thing.

28. A firm comes to the point of shutdown when _______.

A. The total revenue is equal to the total variable cost	**B.** The total revenue is equal to the total cost
C. The marginal cost is equal to the average cost	**D.** The total cost is equal to the average variable cost

Answer: D

Explanation:

The shutdown point denotes the exact moment when a company's (marginal) revenue is equal to its variable (marginal) costs.

29. When the total revenue is greater than the total cost, it is a situation of ______.

A. Normal losses	**B.** Abnormal losses
C. Normal profits	**D.** Abnormal profits

Answer: D

Explanation:

When the total revenue is greater than the total cost, it is a situation of Abnormal profits.

30. A firm makes _____ at the break-even point.

A. Abnormal profits	**B.** Abnormal losses
C. Normal profits	**D.** None of the above

Answer: C

Explanation:

At break-even point, a firm makes normal profits. At this point, total revenue and total cost are equal. Profits are said to be normal when TR=TC or AR=AC.

Chapter – 4   Perfect Competition - Price Determination and simple applications

Market

A market is a machanism or arrangement through which the buyers and sellers of a commodity or service come into contact with one another and complete the act of sale and purchase of the commodity or service on mutually agreed prices.

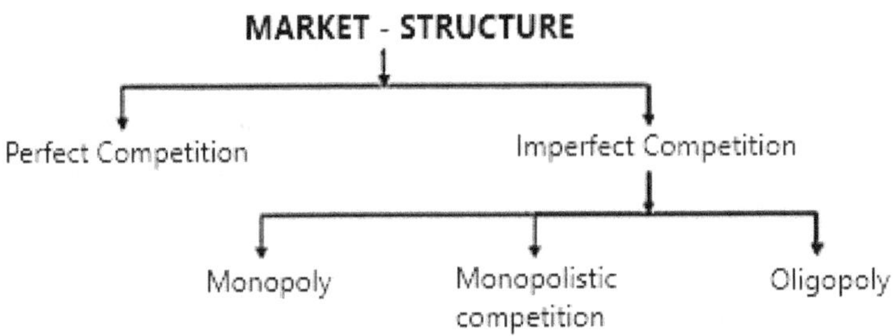

Perfect competition

It is a market structure where there are large number of buyers and sellers selling identical products at uniform price with free entry and exit of firms and absence of govt. control.

Under perfect competition, price remains constant therefore, average and marginal revenue curves coincide each other i.e., they become equal and parallel to X-axis.

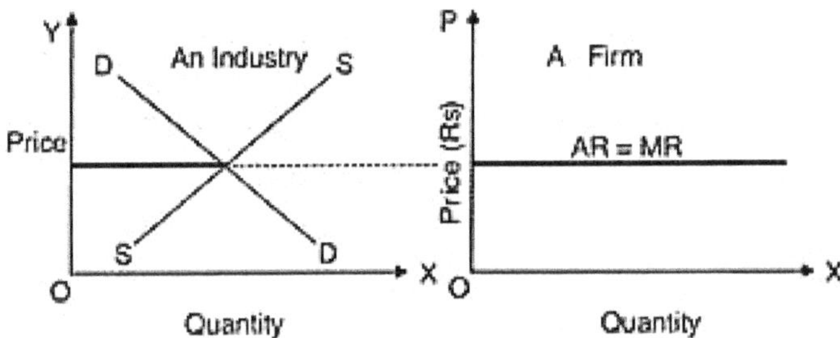

Under perfect competition price is determined by the industry on the basis of market forces of demand and supply. No individual firm can influence the price of the product. A firm can takes the decision regarding the output only. So industry is price maker and firm is price taker.

Feature of perfect competition
- Very large no. of buyers and sellers.
- Homogeneous product.
- Free entry and exit of firms in the market.
- Perfect knowledge.
- Perfect Mobility.
- Perfectly elastic demand curve.
- No transportation cost.

Monopoly market
Monopoly is that type of market where there is a single seller and large number of buyers. There is absence of close substitutes to the products.

Features:
- Single seller and large number of buyers.

- Restrictions on the entry of new firms.
- Absence of close substitutes.
- Full control over price
- Price discrimination.
- Price maker
- Downward sloping less elastic demand curve.

AR or MR Curve in Monopoly market

AR (Demand) Curve slopes downward from left to right and less elastic than that of monopolistic competition. It means that to increase demand, he has to reduce the price.

Given the demand for his product, the monopolist can increase his sales by lowering the price, the marginal revenue also falls but the rate of fall in marginal revenue is greater than that in average revenue.

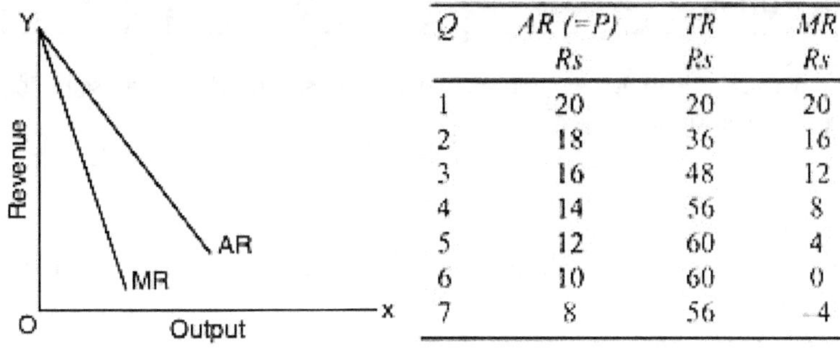

Q	AR (=P) Rs	TR Rs	MR Rs
1	20	20	20
2	18	36	16
3	16	48	12
4	14	56	8
5	12	60	4
6	10	60	0
7	8	56	−4

A monopolist either decides price or output. He cannot decides both at a time.

Market Equilibrium

Market equilibrium is the condition where the production by the sellers and the demand of that product by the buyer becomes equal. We can find the equilibrium price by putting the demand equal to the demand. The equilibrium price is the price at which the quantity demanded equals the quantity supplied.

The demand curve is the curve that depicts the quantity demanded at any price while the supply curve depicts the quantity supplied at any price. So there is one price on the graph that they have in common.

Shifts in Demand and Supply

The law of supply and demand represents the interaction between manufacturers and consumers. This theory shows how these two concepts are interlinked, and the price of a product can affect its sales. The supply-demand curve represents this concept in a graphical manner for better understanding.

Supply and demand law are one of the fundamentals of economics that is related to almost every principle of economics. Moreover, this supply-demand principle also affects the equilibrium prices of a product and often determines its price. However, there are various reasons that can affect this principle.

Shift in Supply Demand Curve

If there are any changes in this curve, it has a direct effect on market equilibrium. Here are some notable factors that can affect supply and demand:

1. Change of Demand

The demand for a product changes due to one of the following factors –
- Population
- Per capita income
- Preferences
- Value of the essential commodities
- Value of substitute items
- Forecast of change in prices

2. Change in Supply

Supply of an item alters owing to the following reasons:

- Number of manufacturers
- Taxes levied
- Technological advancement
- Aim of the companies
- Cost of factors of production
- Cost of competitive products
- Expectation of future price change

This offers a brief idea about the major factors that have an effect on supply and demand. However, to understand this concept in detail, one must understand how a market reacts when both supply and demand curve shifts.

Monopolistic competition

It is that type of market in which there are large number of buyers and sellers. The Sellers sell differentiated product but not identical. The products are close substitutes of each other.

Features

- Large no. of buyers and sellers
- Product Differentiation: The products of each firm is differentiated from the other on the basis of colour, taste, packing, trademark, size and shape.
- Selling Cost: Cost on advertisement and sales promotion.
- Free entry or exit of firms.
- Lack of perfect knowledge.
- Partial control over price.
- Imperfect mobility: Factors of production and products are not perfectly mobile.
- Elastic and downward sloping demand curve.

AR or MR in Monopolist Market

AR (Demand) Curve is left to right downward sloping curve and more elastic / flatter than that of monopoly. It means that in response to change in price, the change in demand will be relatively more for a monopolistic competitive firm than a monopoly firm.

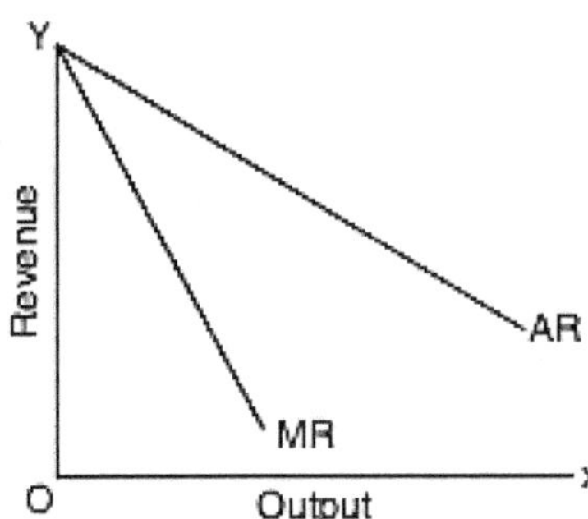

AR and MR curves are both downward sloping because more units can be sold only by lowering the price. MR lies below AR.

Oligopoly

Oligopoly is the form of market in which there are few sellers or few large firms, intensely competing against one another and recognising interdependence in their decision-making.

Features of Oligopoly

- Few Sellers.
- All the firms produce homogeneous or differentiated product.
- Under oligopoly demand curve cannot be determined. It has a kinked demand curve.
- All the firms are interdependent in respect of price determination.

- Price rigidity.

On the basis of production, oligopoly can be categorised in two categories:
- Collusive oligopoly is that form of oligopoly in which all the firms decide to avoid competition and determine the price and quantity of output on the basis of cooperative behaviour.
- Non-collusive oligopoly is that form of oligopoly in which all the firms determine the price and quantity of output according to the action and reaction of the rival firms.

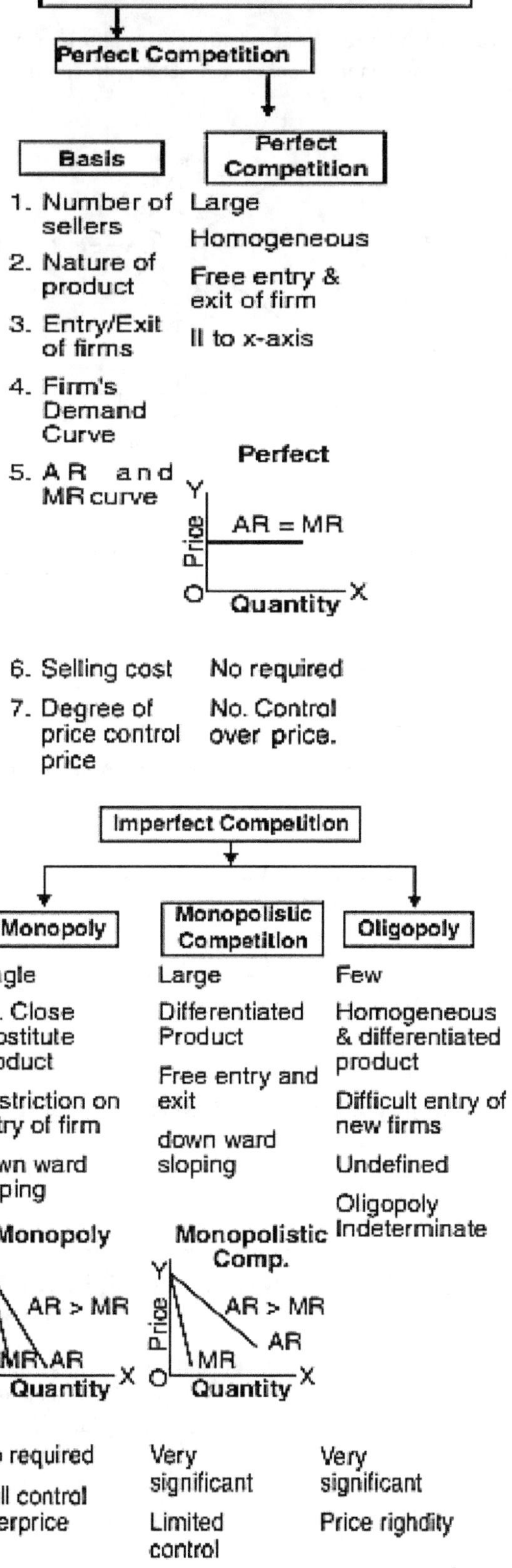

On the basis of product differentiation,Oligopoly,can be categorised in two categories:
- Perfect Oligopoly: The Oligopoly is perfect or pure when the firms deal in the homogeneous products.
- Imperfect Oligopoly: Whereas the Oligopoly is said to be imperfect, when the firms deal in heterogeneous products, i.e. products that are close but are not perfect substitutes.

Equilibrium Price
The price at which the quantity demanded and supplied are equal is known as equilibrium price.

Equilibrium quantity
The quantity demanded and supplied at an equilibrium price is known as equilibrium quantity.

Market equilibrium is a state in which market demand is equal to market supply. There is no excess demand and excess supply in the market.

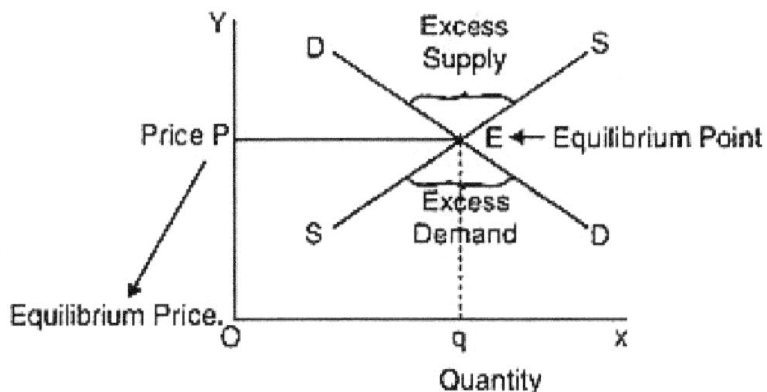

Application of Demand of Supply
- **Maximum Price Ceiling:** It means the maximum price the sellers are allowed to charge less than equilibrium market price. Government imposes such a ceiling when it finds that the demand for necessary goods exceeds its supply. That is, when consumers are facing shortages and equilibrium price is too high. Government does it in the interest of consumers.

Excess demand may be fulfilled by: (a) Rationing (b) Dual marketing

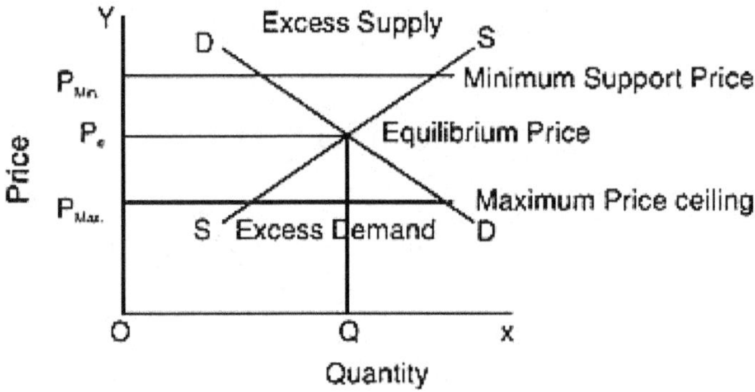

- **Minimum Price Ceiling:** It means that producer are not allowed to sell, the goods below the price fixed by Government, When government finds that equilibrium price is too low for the produce, then Govt. fixes a price ceiling higher than equilibrium price to prevent the possible loss to the producers. The price is also called floor price or minimum support price. Generally, government buys the excess supply at this price.

Multiple Choice Questions

1. ______ is determined when the quantity demanded of a commodity becomes equal to the quantity supplied.
   - A. Market supply
   - B. Market demand
   - C. Market equilibrium
   - D. None of the above

Answer: C

Explanation:

Market equilibrium is determined when the quantity demanded of a commodity becomes equal to the quantity supplied.

2. The price determined corresponding to market equilibrium is known as _____.

    A. Market supply   **B.** Market price

    C. Market demand   **D.** Market equilibrium

Answer: B

Explanation:

The price determined corresponding to market equilibrium is known as Market price .

3. The quantity sold at equilibrium level is known as:

    A. Equilibrium quantity   **B.** Maximum quantity

    C. Quantity supplied   **D.** All of the above

Answer: A

Explanation:

The quantity sold at equilibrium level is known as Equilibrium quantity.

4. Excess supply results in _____.

    A. Surplus   **B.** Competition among sellers

    C. Both A & B   **D.** None of the above

Answer: C

Explanation:

Excess supply results in Surplus and Competition among sellers.

5. Excess demand results in______.

    A. Surplus   **B.** Competition among seller

    C. Both A & B   **D.** Competition among buyers

Answer: D

Explanation:

Excess demand will cause the price to rise, and as price rises producers are willing to sell more, thereby increasing output.

6. Firm is a _____ under Perfect competition.

    A. Price maker   **B.** Price taker

    C. Price influencer   **D.** Price controller

Answer: B

Explanation:

Firm is a Price taker under Perfect competition.

7. Industry under perfect competition is _____.

    A. Price maker   **B.** Price taker

    C. Price influencer   **D.** Price controller

Answer: A

Explanation:

Industry under perfect competition is Price maker.

8. Each firm under market equilibrium earns______.

    A. Supernatural profit   **B.** Negative profit

    C. Normal profit   **D.** None of the above

Answer: C

Explanation:

Each firm under market equilibrium earns Normal profit .

9. ______ is when decisions of consumers and producers in the market are coordinated through the free flow of prices.

    A. Price elasticity   **B.** Price making

    C. Price taking   **D.** Price mechanism

Answer: D

Explanation:

Price mechanism is when decisions of consumers and producers in the market are coordinated through the free flow of prices.

10. _____ operates under market equilibrium.

    A. Law of demand   **B.** Law of supply

    C. Both A and B   **D.** None of the above

Answer: C

Explanation:

A market is in equilibrium if at the market price the quantity demanded is equal to the quantity supplied. The price at which the quantity demanded is equal to the quantity supplied is called the equilibrium price or market clearing price, and the corresponding quantity is the equilibrium quantity.

11. A situation where the quantity demanded is more than the quantity supplied at the prevail marker price is known as;

    A. Excess equilibrium   **B.** Excess demand

    C. Excess supply   **D.** Shortage

Answer: B

Explanation:

Excess demand is a situation when the quantity demanded is more than the quantity supplied at the prevailing market price. The price will start increasing up to the level where there is no excess demand, i.e., Q demanded is equal to Q supplied.

12. In excess demand, buyers are ready to Pay higher prices to:

    A. Sell the excess stock   **B.** Meet their demands

    C. Both A and B   **D.** None of the above

Answer: B

Explanation:

Under the situation of excess demand, consumers would be willing to pay higher prices to meet increased demand. In essence, the price would rise to the equilibrium level.

13. Situation, when the quantity supplied, is more than the quantity demanded at the prevailing market price.

    A. Excess equilibrium   **B.** Excess demand

    C. Excess supply   **D.** Shortage

Answer: C

Explanation:

Excess supply is a market condition when the quantity supplied is greater than the demand for a commodity at the prevailing market price.

14. An industry for which supply curve and demand curve intersect each other in positive axes is known as;

    A. Equilibrium industry   **B.** Viable industry

    C. Non-Viable industry   **D.** All of the above

Answer: A

Explanation:

Equilibrium - Where Demand and Supply Intersect. Because the graphs for demand and supply curves both have price on the vertical axis and quantity on the horizontal axis, the demand curve and supply curve for a particular good or service can appear on the same graph.

15. A demand curves shifts due to:

    A. Change in price of complementary goods   **B.** Change in taste and preferences

    C. Change in population   **D.** All of the above

Answer: D

Explanation:

Demand curves can shift. Changes in factors like average income and preferences can cause an entire demand curve to shift right or left. This causes a higher or lower quantity to be demanded at a given price.

16. Supply curve shifts due to:

    A. Change in the number of firms   **B.** Change in taxation policy

    C. Change in the goals of the firm   **D.** All of the above

Answer: D

Explanation:

Supply curve is shifted due to the change in the supply. An increase in the change in supply leads to the supply curve being shifted to the right, while a decrease in change in supply results in the supply curve shifting to the left.

17. An increase in demand leads to:

    A. Rightward shift   **B.** Leftward shift

    C. Upward movement   **D.** Downward movement

Answer: A

An increase in demand leads to Rightward shift. This could be caused by a number of factors, including a rise in income, a rise in the price of a substitute or a fall in the price of a complement.

18. A decrease in demand leads to:

A. Rightward shift	**B.** Leftward shift
C. Upward movement	**D.** Downward movement

Answer: B

Explanation:
A decrease in demand leads to Leftward shift. That means less of the good or service is demanded. That happens during a recession when buyers' incomes drop. They will buy less of everything, even though the price is the same.

19. The aspects of the market are_____&______.

A. Demand	**B.** Supply
C. Both A & B	**D.** None of the above

Answer: C

Explanation:
The aspects of the market are Demand & Supply.

20. _____ is the nervous system of modern economic life.

A. Market	**B.** Demand
C. Supply	**D.** None of the above

Answer: A

Explanation:
Market is the nervous system of modern economic life.

21. ______ refers to the number and type of firms operating in the industry.

A. Market	**B.** Market structure
C. Commodity sold	**D.** All of the above

Answer: B

Explanation:
Market structure refers to the number and type of firms operating in the industry.

22. ______ refers to a market situation where there are a very large number of buyers and sellers.

A. Oligopoly	**B.** Perfect competition
C. Monopoly	**D.** Monopolistic competition

Answer: B

Explanation:
Perfect competition refers to a market situation where there are a very large number of buyers and sellers.

23. The products in perfect competition are_____ in nature.

A. Heterogeneous	**B.** Differing
C. Homogeneous	**D.** All of the above

Answer: C

Explanation:
The products in perfect competition are Homogeneous in nature.

24. The price in perfect competition is determined by ______.

A. Industry	**B.** A particular firm
C. Buyers	**D.** Sellers

Answer: A

Explanation:
The price in perfect competition is determined by Industry.

25. The factors of production under perfect competition market are _____.

A. Immobile	**B.** Heterogeneous
C. Mobile	**D.** None of the above

Answer: C

Explanation:

The factors of production under perfect competition market are Mobile.

26. Transportation cost under a perfect competition market is ______.
    A. High
    B. Very low
    C. Not determined
    D. Zero

Answer: D

Explanation:

Transportation cost under a perfect competition market is Zero.

27. "Under perfect competition, an individual firm cannot influence the Market price", because:
    A. Absence of selling cost
    B. Absence of transportation cost
    C. The firm is a price taker
    D. None of the above

Answer: C

Explanation:

"Under perfect competition, an individual firm cannot influence the Market price", because The firm is a price taker.

28. "There is the absence of abnormal profit in the long run under perfect competition." What can be the reason for this?
    A. Freedom of free entry and exit
    B. Homogenous products
    C. A very large number of buyers and sellers
    D. Perfect knowledge among buyers and sellers

Answer: A

Explanation:

"There is the absence of abnormal profit in the long run under perfect competition." The reason for this is Freedom of free entry and exit.

29. Which of the following is correct?
    A. The process of charging different prices from different consumers for the same product is called price extension
    B. The process of charging different prices from different consumers for the same product is called price control
    C. The process of charging different prices from different consumers for the same product is called price discrimination
    D. None of the above

Answer: C

Explanation:

The process of charging different prices from different consumers for the same product is called price discrimination.

30. Which of the following is true about the average revenue curve?
    A. The average revenue curve is shaped as a horizontal straight line in a perfect competition
    B. The average revenue curve is shaped as a vertical straight line in a perfect competition
    C. The average revenue curve is shaped downward to the right in a perfect competition
    D. The average revenue curve is shaped rectangular hyperbola in a perfect competition

Answer: A

Explanation:

The average revenue curve is shaped as a horizontal straight line in a perfect competition.